WE CAN'T GO BACK

ROBERT L. HIRSCH

Copyright ©2024 Robert L. Hirsch

This is a work of fiction. All the characters, names, incidents, organizations, and dialogue are either the product of the author's imagination or are used fictitiously.

Published by Harper Book Writers

Other Works by the Author

Invisible Threat

Contents

1

Somewhere in Iran, West of Tehran
2020

Alilah loathed the heat, but her commander pushed her hard in all seasons. Close to 100° F in July, without a cloud in the sky, she needed to demonstrate her capabilities in any situation. Running the last kilometer of ten, she almost caught twice her age, Kurt, until she approached the end of the run and dropped into a lone area of shade. Kurt doubled back a few yards and settled down beside her.

"That was quite a run," Alilah said, panting and rubbing the perspiration off her arms and legs. "I feel like after all of our training and planning, we need to get on with our fight with Israel right now.

Kurt, wiping sweat from his brow and muscular frame, said, "You have no patience. I have told you that our generals around the world are in place and ready to act upon our command. These plans are global."

Alilah knew exactly what Kurt referred to, and now she wondered if she really wanted to be working with him. Kurt was a relatively new partner for her. From her early teen years, she thought and acted quickly to raise money for Islamic terrorists in the States. Now, on the other side of the world, Alilah was called to action. But it was more than a worldwide Intifada. Kurt had more in mind than attacking Israel and the West, both common enemies. But yet here they sat, and he was seemingly stuck in neutral.

As the midday heat intensified even in the shade, Kurt, wiping perspiration off his muscular frame, continued, "You have to keep trusting me. Soon, I will show you what we have built around the globe."

Trust, it develops over a long time, Alilah thought. Or it may never come to pass. Would she ever really believe in Kurt? She thought that he did take her in when on the run from the CIA and FBI. Her husband, the infamous Dr. Alan Mazer, trusted her, but she really never trusted him, even after ten years of marriage. He traveled the world as an Islamic terrorist, deploying dangerous viruses and mutant vaccines that killed thousands of people. Alilah knew what he was doing, but he was clueless about her role. All along, from her early years she enjoyed her role raising funds behind the scenes and helping to finance terrorism. Alan saw her as just an administrator at a mosque and then as a loving mother to his children. It was just safer for the mosque, the family and the enterprise to keep their roles separate and distinct.

Now Kurt brings up plans, always plans, but Alilah knew they were lucky that the Revolutionary Guard and Iranian government had no idea what was going on. She and Kurt had both kept loyal, and Kurt, she knew, paid the government, so they were left alone.

"Yes, Kurt, I know all this already," she said, discouraged, "but to remain undetected, we only communicate indirectly with our colleagues around the globe. We cannot be detected by anyone within Iran or outside of the country. You have to tell me something more. This frustrates me since my goals and those of the Palestinians need to be included."

"Soon, we shall leave Iran and head to inspect the field in person," Kurt said, "at that time, you will see, as I told you, the activities that have been ongoing. I will show you the building and the vast plans in store once the takeover has been completed. Alilah, we must make it clear we are no proxy for Iran. Yes, we sit here undisturbed by the Revolutionary Guard and any arm of the Iranian Government. I have given the utmost respect to the Supreme Leader for decades, and have paid the government handsomely. As such, we have operated freely without any interference."

"Good, now I *very* much look forward to leaving Iran. But please, you must give me some sense or an example of these plans now," Alilah said with still some aggravation in her voice.

"Yes, I will. Many years and much thought have gone into these plans. For example, we will begin a reeducation program for certain classes of persons in the West. Jews, Blacks, Hispanics,

LGBTQ$^+$ and certain others will be sent to retraining labor camps. These labor camps are currently placed at clandestine locations housing a small sample of these undesirable population of persons. The camps will be used to manage agriculture and other needs, but essentially will eliminate this population from our new system," Kurt summarized.

"This sounds like an excellent start," she said aloud.

Alilah did not understand how this plan related to what she envisioned as a military Jihad and her years of study and the last two with Kurt.

"And how will you define a 'pure person' Kurt?"

"Clearly, you and your people have nothing to worry about. But the camps I have described will be the only way to weed out those who do not believe in our new system of government," Kurt concluded.

"And the infrastructure has been built, right?" Alilah asked.

"Yes, much of it; I also have a master plan, just like the Spanish did in the 1400s, to isolate all those of the Jewish faith, all those that befriend them, and other undesirables, such as Blacks and Hispanics." Kurt continued, "It is a huge project and one that needs your attention."

Alilah took a deep breath and sat up straighter to move into more shade. Kurt studied her dark brown eyes curiously. She noticed his stare and, even in the heat, felt a chill.

"I look forward to working with you on all these plans and getting them into action," said Alilah.

"We will, soon enough," said Kurt.

2

Providence, Rhode Island, USA
December 2020

Sarah Rogers, a stunning woman in her later thirties, stood in the kitchen on a beautiful winter's day, thinking that she really could be in her car and rolling out to the mall already. She knew that her husband and son planned to golf since the forecast called for temperatures in the 50s and a beautiful day in December.

"Mike, I have a pretty good feeling you and our son are not doing Christmas shopping today. I have put together a great breakfast for everyone. The stores open at ten, and Avery and I will be there," said Sarah, calling up the stairway, "I am sure you boys don't want to miss your tee time."

In a matter of minutes, the rest of the Rogers crew rolled into the kitchen, apologized to Mom, and dug into waffles, bacon, juice and, for Mike, a large mug of Dunkin Donuts coffee. Sarah could not wait to spend a day shopping with her preteen daughter Avery, and she knew Mike looked forward to any time on the course with their older son, Jon.

"Avery, you will choke if you eat any faster. The stores will wait for us." It would not be long. The two "women" would drive to Providence Place Mall, and within 20 minutes, their fun day would start. Sarah really didn't mind that Mike and Jon would be out on the golf course. She knew it would be packed with other hackers, but he could not resist a mild winter's day on the golf course. The weather might turn on a dime, and it could snow tomorrow. Mike did not procrastinate on his holiday shopping, but he had his priorities. Stores would be open tomorrow, but the greens could easily be snowed under and soon closed for the rest of the season.

Sarah felt her feet aching after several hours of walking and shopping for a long list of friends and family. Avery stopped again, this time in front of the new Hollister store and gazed at an outfit.

"Avery, that does not look very special," said Sarah.

"It's perfect for school. It looks warm, and it is starting to get cold," said Avery.

"I'm exhausted, let's save it for another day. Wait, what was that? Listen!" said Sarah.

A woman ran past them, carrying her young child. They heard several loud popping sounds echoing throughout the mall. Avery looked terrified. They heard more popping sounds coming from overhead. Sarah saw a man grab his midsection and fall to the ground. She took Avery's hand.

"Come on," she said as the pops grew louder. A woman and her son ran past Sarah and Avery. Someone was shouting, "What's going on?"

A young child was crying terribly. Sarah dropped down behind a large concrete planter, pulling Avery with her, shielding her and that same time, trying to cover her daughter's eyes. The popping grew louder, and then Sarah saw a woman grab at her chest. A star of blood appeared, and she fell to the ground.

And as abruptly as it had started, the shooting stopped. Sarah couldn't move, but she could hear Avery softly crying. "Mommy,' Avery said. She hadn't called Sarah that since she was eight years old. Sarah then heard sirens.

Sarah thought, why here, two weeks before Christmas?

Avery, shaking, whispered, "Are we safe now."

"I think so. Let's stay here a while," said Sarah, holding her tight. She heard more and more sirens close by and no additional shooting.

Sarah stood up slowly, keeping Avery on the floor. She saw an unimaginable bloody scene just several feet away in front of storefronts across the lobby. Although she knew she would, she only hoped that the spectacle did not register in her daughter's mind. Who and what kind of person could do this to innocent people? Why? Tears ran down her face. As Avery pulled at her mom's hand, Sarah picked her off the floor and held her close.

Avery shook but a little less.

When an EMT walked over to check out Sarah and Avery, Sarah immediately asked, "Where did everybody go? I don't see many people," she said in a muted voice.

"As soon as people realized what was happening, everyone in the stores exited the back of the establishments. Those near exits left the mall immediately. Only a few hundred were in harm's way," he said, "How are you both feeling?"

"We are both scared and tired," said Sarah.

"But safe," said Avery.

"Please check out my daughter first, and I want to call my husband. By the way, I am Sarah, and this is Avery Rogers from Barrington, RI. Thank you."

Sarah called Mike's cell phone.

"Mike, I am glad you answered. I need you to come home," Sarah said.

"We are already home. It has been six hours since we left this morning. What's wrong?" he asked.

"There has been a mass shooting at the mall…

"What, are you and Avery okay?" Mike asked.

We are but scared to death. An EMT is just checking us out,

and I am sure we will be home soon," she said.

"My God. I love you. See you soon. I'm so happy you are ok. I will put it on the news. Love you," he said.

"Bye, honey."

"OK she checks out just fine, just a little elevated heart rate and blood pressure for now. That will come down in a bit," he said, "Now, let me give you a quick check."

Sarah left with full packages and an empty heart. She always thought she was safe in her small state and now Sarah felt confused. She and Avery were exposed to stress and suffering for their rather long shopping outing. As they left the mall, they didn't dare look up. They walked quickly to the car and headed home to what she thought was the comfort of their place on the east bay of Rhode Island. She wondered if she should talk to Mike about buying a gun. The thought had never, ever come into her head before.

Sarah's hands were unsteady on the wheel of the car as she drove along I195 toward Barrington, but she could not concentrate on her driving. Her mind kept on returning to the mass shootings in schools, theatres, arenas, marketplaces, and places of worship around most of the Western world. She thought of the recent news of cars and trucks driven by crazed young men and women ramming into public buildings, churches and synagogues, killing innocents. Sarah kept up with the news; the shooters and other attackers, according to investigators, had no known relationships with each other. They did not have prior diagnosed psychiatric issues or membership in extremist organizations. The Federal Bureau of Investigation and international agencies involved could not put together any significant patterns in attacker characteristics or timing of these events.

Sarah could not wait to pull into her street and the driveway.

"I never have been so happy to see you too," said Mike. She opened the car door. Within ten seconds the family golden retriever jumped all over Sarah and Avery, and then a family hug ensued, all gathered around her car.

"I have news for you. Jon and I have been watching the television coverage since you called. It looks like there was one lone shooter. He was perched on the top floor of the mall," he said, "The shooter was taken down by an off-duty Providence City Police Officer."

"We were so lucky to be out of range. You and I will have to discuss follow-up care for me and Avery. This event was unimaginable," Sarah said.

"The loss of life and serious injuries reported overwhelmed the area hospitals, thirty-five persons were killed and 78 seriously wounded. Many had to be transported to Boston and Worcester," Mike said.

"Well, I can't go back to that mall again. Mike, I do not want to hear any more details," Sarah said, and then she walked quickly into the house.

3

Congressional House Select Committee
June 2020

Crime, Terrorism and Homeland Security Committee, Closed Session:

Congressman Kenneth Carlin, Maryland, Chairperson:

"Colonel Ickerson, or as others may know you as Dr. Arnold Ickerson, CEO of Immunoviratherapeutics, I wish to thank you for your opening statement on behalf of your Company. We all thank you for your prior service to the country in the war on terrorism. We know the good that your Company tried to accomplish with its vaccines. That was almost two years ago now. Things do move slower in the halls of Congress than we like to admit. Now we face a different battle. Under your watch and those of your employees, a terrorist inflicted great harm with the Company's new measles vaccine, MVoneshot. Thousands of children and teens died here and around the world. Was this just a one-off "Super-Tylenol" crisis coming from al-Queda or another terrorist organization, or are there more attacks yet to come?"

"The Joint Terrorist Task Force has investigated your Company and knows of at least one in-house collaborator. However, Congress will dig for itself, which is why we are convened here today. How can such an intrusion into a U.S. corporation occur? This is not a computer hack, from our understanding. How does a company allow such an event to occur? What oversight does the FDA have after the approval of a new biological agent or drug? It sounds on the surface to this Committee that an 'FDA person in the plant' might be a permanent consideration for the future. The FDA and the JTTF will also be testifying before this Committee in this session. These are a few of the questions my colleagues will have for you. We will begin with opening statements from the FDA and then the Company. After each presentation the Committee will question each presenter. We will start with Dr. Fredericka Lansing, Director of the Center for Biologics Evaluation and Research within the FDA, Dr. Lansing…."

4

Escaping Trouble: Baltimore to Boston
July 2019

Sabina knew her husband, Dr. Alan Mazer, continued to be a poor communicator. When he had not returned home that night, she just assumed he had another hospital emergency or chose again to work in his laboratory all night. That was not unusual. For years she only saw him between his priority work, patients, or international trips. Sabina didn't think he saw their children but once a week. She had not felt close to him or good about their marriage for several years.

Then Sabina saw his face. As soon as she saw Alan on the television news at Dulles Airport, as he was taken into custody, her palms grew sweaty. She almost dropped her coffee mug but did manage to place it trembling into the sink before spilling its contents. Sabina now steadied herself momentarily and recognized immediately this was time for the action plan. The plan developed by the Imam long ago in the event any problems arose required quick implementation and exit from the country.

Alan, a radicalized Muslim, had just been arrested for trying to escape the United States using a false identity. He was taken into custody for murdering a colleague in his lab. The bigger news- his alleged role in the planning and implementation of a terrorist attack with a mutated measles vaccine several months previously. He introduced it into the market, killing and injuring thousands of innocent children and young teens around the world. She had to wonder why the murder? Why did he set himself up to run now?

Sabina recognized that something like this could happen at any time, and action was needed immediately. She appreciated that authorities would question her. Alan carried out the attacks with a collaborator inside a biotechnology company, Immunoviratherapeutics, yet her husband Alan never knew Sabina raised funds for terrorist activities. She knew her role as a key money raiser was under deep cover. In any case, Sabina hated the idea of being questioned as the wife of a captured terrorist.

"Kids," she yelled up the stairs of the condo, "We are going on an adventure to see Jidi and Papi in Boston."

Sabina knew her parents, Jidi and Papi, remained oblivious to her role in supporting military Jihad activity and coordinating programs with the Imam at the Baltimore Mosque. She remembered her first big lie as a teenager when she went to 'France' as an exchange student in high school but, without regret had spent the whole semester in Libya.

"Aamir, bring down the 'bug-out-bag' under your bed," said Sabina.

"Okay Mom," said Aamir.

The 'bug out bag' packed with clothes, food, water and medicine for her and her children lay under his bed. Sabina knew she could leave at a moment's notice with that bag.

"Aamir, Najah," she said, "Where are you? I am ready to go and I do not see you downstairs."

"Coming," they said in unison as the two seven-year-olds bounded down the stairs with small backpacks in their hands.

"Aamir, do you have the bug-out bag?" asked Sabina.

"Yes, I put it in my backpack," he said.

"Good. Najah, I have some other candy and protein bars. Let me put them in your bag," she said.

"Here Mom," said Najah, as she held open a zipper compartment of her backpack.

"Thanks, honey,"

"We now begin our big adventure. Let's go to the car," said Sabina.

"Are we driving? We should fly. It's a long trip to Jidi's house," said Aamir.

"I know, and last minute on a weekend, I could not get three seats on the plane. Daddy called me to say he was busy all weekend," she lied, "So let's drive. It will be fun."

Thinking to herself how much 'fun' this ride might be, Sabina realized she first needed to change her car. She took her first detour before leaving Baltimore and headed to the mosque where she worked as an administrator ever since Alan had started at a top-notch Baltimore hospital years ago.

"Imam, I am so happy I caught you before 'Asr prayer time," said Sabina, "I need to speak with you about an urgent matter. Children, could you go into my office over there and just draw on the whiteboard for a few minutes. Thanks."

After a pause, he began. "Sabina, I have seen the news. I know what happened and what must be done. I have sent word to several sources to get things moving to help you," he said, "You remain a key member of our community, and we need you to remain safe. I have reservations for you to fly to France tomorrow night from Boston. I figured you would go to your parent's home. From Paris, other plans are already in development. Your new identity and all other papers are in this envelope. You will find some Euros in here as well. Go now and be safe."

"Imam, you have been so kind and helpful, but I must ask for one more thing. I think it wise that I switch cars on my trip to

Boston and use one of the vehicles from the mosque. You may keep mine and the registration," she said.

"Of course. I should have thought of that myself. Peace be upon you and your little ones," said the Imam. The Imam pulled a key from his pocket and gave it to her.

"May Allah reward you," she said. Sabina collected her two children and left immediately.

Sabina did not like the idea of traveling on the interstate highways, so she headed to U.S. Route 1. She thought her chance of being spotted by a state trooper, even in a different car, was greater than the risk of being caught on surveillance cameras on local roads. She could not imagine anyone looking for the mosque's car on these local cameras now. She understood the typical trip on the highways lasted eight hours or so, and by this route, it might be a twelve-hour grind, with stop lights, strip malls and the like.

Sabina recognized an important call she needed to make on her way north. "Hi, Mom," said Sabina.

"So nice to hear your voice, ya asal (honey). We usually talk earlier in the evening," said Mother.

"The day got away. I just wanted to tell you a surprise. The twins and I are on our way to see you and Dad. Alan is tied up all weekend at an out-of-town conference, so we will be there by morning," said Sabina. She felt uneasy as she spoke these untruths to her mother, and she gripped the wheel tighter.

"By morning. What do you mean? Are you driving?" she asked.

"Yes. This is all a last-minute getaway. And I will tell so much more later. I will be there in the mid-morning. I plan to be off to France for the weekend. I hope you can watch the kids." Sabina said with an inflection at the end of her sentence, as if it were a question.

"France, my goodness. I wish I had more notice. But I am happy to care for Aamir and Najah and cannot wait to see you all," said her mother.

"Don't worry. The kids are excited to see you and Dad. Bye-bye Mom. I have to concentrate on driving at night," and Sabina rang off.

Sabina began to question herself on how smoothly the ride had gone. The kids slept quietly in the back, and nothing but smooth sailing, she thought. Then, she noticed the gas gauge slowly edging toward Empty as she crossed the Connecticut- Rhode Island border. And then, she looked in her rear-view mirror on this stark part of Route 1, and her anxiety spiked even higher. She saw a police cruiser coming up fast. She slowed down well below the speed limit, and then the cruiser zipped passed her. Sabina, who unknowingly had held her breath, let out a gasp. She shook visibly.

Just several minutes later, Sabina heard her car begin to sputter loudly as the gas tank was almost completely empty. She pulled off an exit in Narragansett, RI, one of the thickly settled towns in southern Rhode Island, with many stores, restaurants, gas stations, truck stops and fast-food restaurants. She knew she could not refill her car with gas. Sabina had already weighed over the idea that she could have appeared on television news, and anyone might now identify her. Sabina thought it best to dump the car somewhere on route and then find a way to her childhood home north of Boston for the final leg of the trip.

Close to the large state university, she parked the car in a restaurant lot. Before grabbing her kids from their deep sleep in the back seat, Sabina weighed her next step and transformed herself into a conservative Muslim woman. She donned a hijab head covering, which she knew would protect her somewhat from immediate identification. Now, she felt she could start to look for a ride north to Boston. It did not take long for her to find that ride.

"Excuse me," Sabina said as she saw a young man walking toward his car, "I see you have New Hampshire license plates. By any chance, are you traveling north? I could pay for your gasoline."

"Yes, in fact, I am. I am not in the habit of picking up hitchhikers, but I do not think you and your little ones can do me much harm. I am going home for the weekend. Where are you from, and where are you going?" said the young man.

His question bothered Sabina a bit. Was he, in fact, aware of her husband and that now authorities might be looking for a lone Muslim woman? He was a young university kid, just getting off work from the around-the-clock clam shack in the early morning hours.

"We live in Baltimore but are going back home to Revere, Mass, just north of Boston. My parents live there. My name is Sabina and these are my two children, still quite sleepy," she said. Then she thought, I just gave my real name, and from where I was coming. If he really did know the news, I might be in trouble.

"Patrick," he said, "Nice to meet you. I can bring you right to Revere. I know the beach and have been there many times in my high school days."

"That is so kind of you. Thank you. Let me get my children's car seats and bring them to your car. My husband will take care of my car in the morning," Sabina said. "You do not know how thankful I am."

On the ninety-minute ride from southern Rhode Island to Revere, Sabina mulled over the mistakes she made. She hoped that nothing was catastrophic and that Patrick had no clue as to the landscape of the current news.

Sabina hated lying to her own parents but had done it again, telling them that she was coming here since Alan had an out-of-town conference and that she was planning to meet a friend in France from her high school year overseas. She had never been to France for any high school event. The timing would be perfect if her parents could watch the children for a few days. They agreed and would love any time with her and the children.

Now, she finally had some time to look at what the Imam had prepared for her escape. She felt a sense of relief that he booked her on the earliest flight out of Logan to Paris, an Air France flight at 5:20 PM. And, of course, the mosque booked the flight under the name of a French citizen with similar features to Sabina, for which she now held a passport, provided by the Imam.

Sabina was not in any way tied to her husband's crime, but she felt sick that the authorities would be looking for her in a very short time. She hoped that the Imam's plan, sending her to Tehran via Paris and reconnecting with allies in Iran, would work. Sabina felt she had to connect with her network or one with the same goals. The group with which she worked, she thought, had to believe in a global Intifada that justified the use of violence as a means to an end.

Clearly, most Muslims did not follow or believe in the philosophy of al-Qaeda and ISIS fighters, but these factions were currently expanding their network in the United States, Africa and the Middle East.

Sabina had plenty of cash resources squirreled away to tide her over. Upon arrival at her childhood home, Sabina got out of the car and took a deep, cleansing breath. She unbuckled the children's seat belts, and the kids jumped out of Patrick's old Toyota and hugged her mother. Sabina took a long look at her parents' home, the one in which she was raised, and then she tried to pull herself together. Then she grabbed her bags from Patrick's car.

Her mother ran to her and gave her a huge squeeze, and Sabina did the same.

"It has been so long. I miss you so much," said Jidi, the name the kids knew her as.

"I know, Mom, we have been extremely busy, the kids are seven years old now and starting 2nd grade. Alan has been so wrapped up in this research and clinic. I have been crazy with the kids and working with the Imam," Sabina explained, "It has been impossible to take a real vacation. This is my one chance to get away for a bit. Hold on one second."

Sabina turned and walked back to the street where Patrick, the student who drove them, waited in his car. She removed the car seats and thanked him again for the ride. He had driven them all the way from the southernmost part of Rhode Island to north of Boston. She then handed him a crisp fifty-dollar bill. He was very appreciative, and of course, he still needed a shower from the smelly clam shack. She thanked him again and waved goodbye as he headed off to his home.

The children ran by both Jidi and Sabina and flew into the arms of Papi, the muscular grandfather. He squeezed them both until it almost hurt.

"It's about time you arrived here, Sabina. How long are you in town?" he said.

"Actually, just for the lunch and a little longer. I have to run to Logan and catch a flight to Paris, I told Mom last night. I have an early flight, so I could sleep on the plane, and I need it after last night. When I land, Alice Germaine will pick me up, and I will be fresh and ready to see the sights," she explained.

"Well, you can take me too," her dad laughed.

"I would, but this is just for the girls; next time, okay Dad?" Sabina answered.

Her Dad turned and jogged toward the den where Aamir and Najah had already taken out a huge jigsaw puzzle, dumped the pieces on the coffee table, and then spread some of them on the floor.

Papi got on the floor on his back and started acting just like a happy grandpa should. Holding up Najah above his head, he flew her over his head with one hand, landed her on the ground and then picked up Aamir and did the same. Take-offs and landings continued for quite some time. The jigsaw puzzle remained dumped on the floor for now as the kids played with the little hair left on Papi's head.

Sabina felt the next few hours drag on before she needed to leave for the airport. Thankfully, to Sabina's welcome surprise, a major natural disaster in California took the media by storm. Fires across the northern parts of the state-dominated the national news coverage. And even better yet, she realized, after all, the story of Alan's arrest would be largely local because of the murder in Baltimore.

The vaccine problem had existed for months. Sabina, feeling like she was on the run for almost 24 hours, and her parents, not the kind to be online much at all, had yet to hear any news. She felt good that she would be in the air by the time the evening news would cover any of the events and could not wait to get out of the house through passport control and security.

Sabina never exhibited outward anxiety, but her intestines rumbled now. Her head also throbbed as she began to feel the strains of the last two years. Her husband had been the key figure initiating two virus attacks on the world in the past two years. One virus attacked the Israeli delegation in Jordan at the Olympic Games, and one mutated measles vaccine targeted teens and children in a worldwide attack but mostly concentrated in the U.S. As soon she exited the United States, she felt she would be safe. Her children would be secure and protected by her parents.

Sabina planned her departure for 3:00 PM and began hugs and goodbyes just before her Uber driver arrived. Her kids barely waved at her, but her parents were not pleased. They had only a few hours with their daughter, but they knew they would have time with Sabina upon her return.

"I will see you in just a few days," said Sabina, "We will have plenty of time then, as I have no rush to get back to Baltimore. Love you. Thank you so much." She hugged both her mother and father, and just then, the Uber driver pulled up right on time.

She did not look at her watch but noted and was thankful no heavy traffic slowed the route to the airport. She figured the ride to Logan took only 20 to 25 minutes. Sabina's heart raced as she approached Air France counter with her new false identity, the French passport provided by the Imam. To her thankful surprise, she sailed through the passport checking and boarding pass printing process smoothly, but she wondered if this was how she would feel every step she took.

Next Sabina anticipated security and then eventually boarded. She started to debate with herself the wisdom of her ever leaving; first, her husband, who she really had given up on, but now her children, who she loved dearly.

Sabina, annoyed in the long security checkpoint line, began to get a look at everyone as if they were staring at her. She felt her heart racing, and her breathing rate increased. Was she paranoid, or did all these passengers recognize her as the wife of the alleged terrorist and murderer, Dr. Alan Mazer. Sabina finally got to the TSA agent at the front of the line. He looked over her boarding pass and passport and waved her through. Sabina took a deep breath and walked down the lane to place her backpack on the conveyer belt.

Sabina felt so much better. She waited just 30 minutes in the coach lounge before boarding. She was thankful the Imam bought economy plus seats, splurging for the seven-plus hour flight. She thought that maybe the Imam had bought these seats for her comfort on the plane, given that she had raised millions of dollars for Jihad in America.

5

To A New Land

July 2019

Sabina had a restless night. Her husband, the now infamous Dr. Mazer, had been the traveler of the family. She watched in awe as he went around the world and recruited those who would help him set up virus attacks in Jordan and the United States. Sabina on her first trip East since a high school student, felt anxious to get to her final destination. She had a rough time falling asleep as the airplane noise and chatter of so many people in the cabin bothered her. She thought to herself that she must ditch her iPhone before getting to the airport and did so under the car mat on her Uber ride.

Now, with nothing to distract her, the noises seemed louder in her head. Finally, after getting to cruising altitude, the cabin lights on the wide-body jet came full on for 90 minutes as the flight attendants served a less-than-desirable meal, and Sabina felt less tense. After the trays were cleared Sabina feared more noise and distraction, but the lights lowered. She tossed and turned and tried to watch a rom-com movie. She did not prepare for this flight or a new life; this was not a holiday. She missed her children. After several hours, Sabina finally fell asleep.

As the Air France jet touched down, Sabina awoke with a start from her short sleep. She rubbed her eyes and then checked her seat back. She did not bring much with her; other than her backpack with three days of clothes, she was ready to disembark. The plane held for a few minutes and then pulled up to a gate. But the doors remained closed.

The pilot came on the intercom and made an announcement, "Ladies and Gentlemen, Madame's and Monsieur's, it appears that there may be a problem with one of the passengers. Please remain in your seats. We will need to attend to this problem quickly. Thank you for your understanding, Merci."

Sabina kept her head down for a minute and then looked up. Four gendarmes and two men from Interpol rushed down the aisle. Her pulse quickened, and she felt nauseous. Could the authorities be looking for her? Did they know of her relationship with Alan, even though she was carrying false papers? They buzzed several rows right past her. Sabina relaxed almost immediately, but her stomach still felt knotted. In a matter of minutes, four passengers were handcuffed, stood up and pulled out of the plane…drug mules. A Mexican cartel had begun to send fentanyl in human carriers to Europe through the United States. Sabina took several deeper breaths and began to relax.

The captain came on the intercom one more time, "Sorry for the disturbance. I do hope you enjoyed the flight, if not the beginning of your time here in France. Please accept my deepest apologies for the delay. Welcome to France. Good morning. Bon Jour."

Passengers in the cabin ahead of Sabina started to stand and began to deplane. Sabina felt exhausted, not just from the lack of sleep but the terror, thinking that the police were coming for her. She rose from her seat and left the plane. After exchanging some dollars for additional Euros at a kiosk, Sabina headed to a shop to pick up a burner phone. She needed some form of communication, even though it would be one way. Fatigued, she stopped at a small cafe before heading to her next flight and rested comfortably, stretching out while drinking her coffee. Sabina contemplated her next long flight before she could settle in at her final destination.

She did not intend to meet anyone named Alice Germaine, the bogus name she gave her parents upon departure. No Parisian tourist sites were on Sabina's itinerary. After feeling fully caffeinated, mostly sharp and attentive, she headed toward Terminal 2A. Sabina's next twenty-hour adventure began with a scheduled direct flight departing at 6 PM local time, a flight to Istanbul. Her final destination with arrival the following day was Tehran.

The clock on the wall reminded Sabina of third grade in the early afternoon. The hands seemed to stand still as she could not wait for the end of the school day to play with her friends. In this case, the personal stakes grew by the minute. As Sabina sat and drank her coffee, she now realized her husband was the number one worldwide news story. Splashed on the large screens in the cafes and across the hall in the pub, she could see the face of Dr. Alan Mazer. Reported in the French language here, which Sabina understood and translated in English subtitles for international visitors, she only hoped her face did not appear. They reported that he was held for the murder of a colleague and for terrorist activity related to the distribution of a dangerous vaccine.

She watched the overnight news repeated over and over on the giant television screens in the airport, and so far, even though she kept her head down, her face did not appear. The longer she remained in France, despite her new identity, the possibility that she could be picked up by Interpol or French police increased significantly.

Now 2:48 PM local time, Sabina felt exhausted despite the caffeine intake, and this was only the beginning of her journey. She finally pushed the chair back from her third restaurant of the day and headed toward her rendezvous point just outside the Turkish Airlines departure terminal. On a round leather bench in the center of the ticketing area sat a middle-aged woman with a light-complexioned face. She wore a conservative tesettur style scarf and a long, coverall top coat. Sabina took a seat near the woman. This specific location had been included in the package of materials the Baltimore Imam had provided Sabina previously, along with tickets and IDs. Such plans always had been in place.

The right buttons, so to speak, needed to be pushed to activate her exit plan, as they would be for any ally in trouble. Sabina, as per her instructions from the Imam, sat at the table, and placed both of her hands on the table with her thumbs touching and fingers spread. Immediately, the anonymous woman slipped an envelope from her drab brown handbag and slid it on the bench toward Sabina. She knew now, without any doubt this woman was her contact. She took the envelope, placed it in her backpack and walked directly to the nearest restroom. Not a word exchanged, Sabina knew her journey could continue.

Sabina took a seat in the last stall and locked the door. No one had followed her into this rest area and the room had not been particularly crowded since most people scurried toward their departure gates. She ripped open the envelope and found her next set of identity papers and a roundtrip ticket from Paris to Tehran. The package contained her new Turkish passport, including the stamped visa showing an entry into France the week before, and a receipt for a used ticket from Istanbul. Sabina Mazer's new identity was Alilah Cetin (bright tough). Immediately Sabina, now Alilah, thought to herself that she must live up to her new name. She put her old documents, shredded by hand as best she could, into the envelope that had contained the new documents.

On exiting the restroom, "Alilah" tossed the envelope mixed with paper towels from her hand washing into a large trash container. Alilah noted that the woman at the table had disappeared. Now time moved more quickly. It was 3:35, and her flight to Tehran via Istanbul departed at 6:00 PM local time. Just a few more hours and rest would come more easily.

6

Home Again In Langley
February 2021

Nari Lee understood that violence never ceased for Israelis. She knew attacks had been all too common for years in Tel Aviv, all around Gaza, Haifa, and in the north near the Lebanese border. But, now gangs of Hamas terrorists, trained by Hezbollah to the north, squeezed into all areas of the country like never before. Nari and her group did not feel particularly worried this week in the old city of Acre, where they were scouting out information from prior intelligence reports. However, wars on several fronts in Asia and Eastern Europe, as well as natural disasters, pushed people to wherever they could find a place to survive, and Israel welcomed immigrants all over the country.

Just then Nari took several rounds directly to her midsection and upper right quadrant. She fell hard against the rock wall and crumbled to the dirt floor. She knew she should not have been on this assignment. Nari, just months out of her accelerated training at the "farm" in Camp Peary, Virginia, never really intended to be recruited for field action. She had been trained in the sciences, immunology and virology. She thought her education and background would lead to a high-level forensic or virology lab assignment overseas. Her close friend, Martin Erlich, previously head of the Joint Terrorist Task Force, became Director of the CIA.

Thanks to Martin, Nari not only had the pull to get her pushed through training, but he got her this field assignment within months as opposed to years. If she waited much longer, he told her, she would be too old to qualify for any overseas fieldwork. She saw blood spattered on the wall and floor next to her and Special Agent John Walker at her side. "Hell of a first field assignment," …that was her last thought as she lost consciousness.

Nari felt so cooped up during her recovery in Germany. She wondered if she could stay restrained much longer, as she marked each day off the calendar. It was difficult for her to understand that she had only been in the hospital four months. When she heard two more months of rehab in the States were required, Nari became agitated. She felt ready to go back to work and did not want to stay off the job. But she knew she had connections at Langley.

She definitely felt strong enough to get back to the office. Three months in the field gave her a good sense of what that line of work would be like. In retrospect, she thought to herself, why did she really need to do that? Why did she request that field assignment? Sort of late to be asking these dumb questions, having been shot in the chest and abdomen by Hamas in Israel. Then she wondered why Israel? Of course, she knew why. How many women with a Korean background spoke fluent Hebrew? Her parents wanted her to go to the best day school in the Stanford area, so why not a Jewish day school. It was close to their house, she could learn a third language, and the school had a late pick-up time of 6 PM. Perfect for two up-and-coming immigrant parents in the computer field with a start-up company. So, for grades K through 6, Nari enjoyed the company of local Jewish and many non-Jewish kids in the Stanford Beth Sholom Day School.

Not only did she receive a great early education, but that decision really paid off in spades for Nari's CIA career. She received a 'great' field position in Tel Aviv with the CIA. She could sit in a cafe and, as an American-born Korean, overhear Hebrew speakers, and no one would be the wiser. She picked up some Arabic as well. But, on the other hand, who would know that on her very first overseas assignment, she would be sent home riddled with bullets. And, now every time she went through airport security, the one bullet lodged somewhere deep inside her chest would get Nari a secondary scan.

"Nice to have you back early, of course. I hope you first checked in with your new boss," said Martin Erlich.

Who would that be?" Nari asked.

"Michael Hardy, Deputy Director, Intelligence and Analysis. He has been with the Agency for quite a while and is highly regarded. Check in with him immediately after your visit with me, Nari," said Martin.

"Okay. Now, one thing. My preference after the Israel 'thing' would be to stay at Langley and use my strengths analyzing data," Nari said, "Field work may not be such a great fit for me."

"A discussion point for your boss. But as you know, as a tri-lingual, speaking Korean, Hebrew and English, your type is difficult to find and can be deployed in many places," Erlich said.

"Of course, but I'm just putting out the fact that bullets in the abdomen and chest are not the way I expected to start my career," said Nari, "I am open to anything, so let me go down the hall and introduce myself to Michael Hardy and find my desk. It's good to be back."

"Thanks Nari," said Erlich, and he stood up from behind his desk as she left his office.

7

Flight To A New Future

July 2019

Alilah, the former Sabina Mazer, could not believe she was about to board another flight. As she finally heard the general call for coach boarding for the flight to Tehran, her last trip on what seemed like an endless quest, she stood warily and walked to the gate. By following flights that had departed earlier in the day, Alilah knew this was a short flight of only three and a half hours. As she entered the plane, she took her window seat toward the rear of the cabin and quickly fell asleep. She just did not have the energy to even think about what she might have left behind, her beautiful twins, Aamir and Najah. As for her husband, he had been a lost personal cause for years.

At this point, she had now been traveling for close to 2 days, driving from Baltimore to Boston, dropping off her twins with her parents for a "quick trip" to Paris. Then, off to Istanbul with a new identity before anyone might recognize her as the wife of Alan Mazer. Having now boarded her last flight on her arduous trip to Tehran, Alilah would meet an unknown party, all arranged in advance by her contacts in the Muslim world in the West.

Alilah's arrival in Iran was unlike most persons deplaning a flight from Turkey or for that matter a flight from any foreign land. Tehran's Imam Khomeini International Airport was inconveniently located 30 kilometers southwest of Tehran, and traffic to the city could be miserable. Once in the passport control queue, it usually took at least an hour to weave through the line of arriving passengers unless, of course, one had a good connection. Alilah did not know it when she entered the passport control area, but she did have such a connection. She was spotted by a well-dressed man. He pointed to her in the long queue waiting to get through, and then an officer pulled Alilah out of the long and winding line and brought her to the passport control desk. At that point, her pulse raced, and she had no idea what was happening.

A man leaned over from the front of the desk and whispered to her, "My name is Kurt, don't worry, all is well."

As it was, all turned out just perfectly. The passport officer gave her Turkish papers and visa a momentary glance, a stamp and passed her documents back. Alilah's pulse slowed. He then waved Alilah through the checkpoint.

Alilah, with nowhere else to go, slowed her breathing, which had quickened inside and followed this man Kurt through the customs lobby to his car. He opened the door to his large Mercedes parked illegally in front of the airport. Alilah noted that no one stopped her at customs with her backpack, nor questioned Kurt in the restricted area. His car had not been disturbed. She figured he was about 50 years of age.

After they both were in the vehicle Kurt spoke, "Alilah, my name is Kurt Huette. Your Imam in Baltimore and others have arranged for me to pick you up and for us to meet and work together." He then took off out of the airport exit.

"Thank you so much, Kurt. I have had an exhausting and upsetting two days. My husband has been arrested, and I have left my children behind in the States," she said, "We need to understand each other and what we will be doing, but right now, I am physically and emotionally drained."

"I understand," Kurt said, "sit back, I will say as little as possible."

"No, please talk. I will listen. Just do not find me rude if I do not respond," she said.

Kurt, it seemed to Alilah really did like to talk. She thought her preamble would have given him pause, but he told several stories on their ride to his estate, just east of Karaj. She had no idea where that city was located and she really did not know or care at this time.

"Look to the right," Kurt startled her, "There sits an old synagogue. Thousands of Jews still remain right here in Iran even as the government here denies the Holocaust and the right of Israel to exist."

Alilah thought if after centuries of oppression, Iran could not still get rid of all of the Jews, who is this Kurt, and why are we teamed up now. She looked at his face as he drove and saw a man who could easily be Persian, yet he spoke fluent English with no accent.

Kurt kept on speaking in his smooth voice, and now all Alilah could think about was a shower and a change of clothes. She felt disgusting. They did not talk much as Alilah dosed off quickly. When she awoke, they entered a large estate, unlike any homes she could see in the immediate area. Kurt saw her open her eyes, and started to speak again, telling her that his father built the home in the late 1940's, before any other houses had been built here. Now, he was the second generation to live in this home, and he had continued to build on the property. He also built a beach home on the Caspian Sea about two hours north of here. He indicated it was a great spot to get away from city life.

She thought, 'Are we there yet; we drove into his place ages ago,' sounding like her kids. "I am very confused right now. You pick me up at the Tehran Airport. You must know that I am not Turkish, as I'm speaking perfect American English. What is your relationship to me; to those who helped get me here?" she asked.

"Truthfully, it is a long, long story and goes back over 100 years," Kurt said," my name is Kurt Huette. For now, you need to get cleaned up and rest. Then you need to eat; get some of our good local nourishment. And after that, we need to buy you some clothing."

"You are so right, I have just a few things in my backpack and these filthy clothes I am wearing," she said. "I have to trust you. I have come with nothing but my principles and ideas from the past. I do not really know where I am or who you are," Alilah came on strong although weak and tired, "But, I do recognize one thing. What I have worked on for many years has not been completed. I hope we have the same goals, to continue the battle started in America."

As they finally arrived at the front of his home, resembling a large estate, Kurt continued to speak, "I and our many colleagues around the world know about the battles and about the virus attacks which your husband, Dr. Mazer, perpetrated. My Middle East sources tell me other imponderable and catastrophic virus plans started well before Dr. Mazer went to prison. And I, too, have very long-term plans and ideas which I hope we can share.... plans and ideas for Jihad. Israel and the Jews are our common enemy. You might not even realize some plans your husband initiated but did not yet see to their end."

Alilah now felt a bit more relaxed. She anticipated hearing Kurt's family story and how they came to Iran. But now she wanted to take her long-awaited hot shower to wash off the dirt and grime of her ordeal to arrive here. They exited the car and entered his home. She could not believe she was on the other side of the world with a total stranger ready to begin a new life. What would happen next and what she would learn about Kurt and his background would change her future, the strategies for plans against the West, and whatever else this man had in mind.

Kurt pointed to the stairway, "Why don't you take that shower now and get changed. You can have the whole second floor to yourself. My room and study are on this floor."

"Thank you. I desperately need to wash after the last two days of travel. Thank you," said Alilah.

As she walked up the ornate stairway, Alilah could not quite grasp how she found herself in this remote part of Iran in this wealthy man's home. Why not some Middle East country closer to the action. She realized she had been at a desk raising money and her kids. Yes, Iran funded much of the anti-Israeli bombing and attacks through proxies. But, as she approached her room, confused as ever, she thought she would be better off in someplace like Lebanon or Syria, where she could interact directly with militants. Who was this Kurt Huette?

In her shower, Alilah could not let go of her thoughts and anxiety despite her exhaustion. Where did Kurt Huette really come from? Kurt told her on the drive that he was a child of the 60s and his father was of German descent. His dark hair and complexion gave away that his mother must have been Persian. No wonder, she now remembered, he spoke such fluent Farsi as he walked through the airport. But still, an unease curled in her stomach. She wasn't sure why she should trust him. At least not yet.

Alilah, while drying off, finally started to relax. She tried to understand why but then decided why bother. She put on whatever she had in her backpack, a cutoff pair of jean shorts and a t-shirt, and toweled off her short hair. Exhausted, Alilah laid herself out on the bed and did not come downstairs until early the next day.

Alilah was surprised when she saw Kurt standing ready at the front doorway, acting like a guard.

"Something wrong," she said.

"Not at all. Ready for an early morning run?" he asked, "I have water for you if you got enough rest last night."

"Let's do it. My running shoes could use replacement soon, but these will work for now," said Alilah. She really wanted to know why she ended up here in the middle of Iran, but that information would have to wait. Alilah, although a criminal herself, felt uncomfortable not knowing who was keeping her and with whom she was making these new plans.

That evening, the two of them enjoyed a wonderful, authentic Persian meal.

Alilah said, "Kurt, first you must tell me about the main course. Did you prepare this and second, it is delicious. What are these dishes?"

"Well, you might have guessed I do have some Persian heritage. The rice side dish is called tahchin. It is a savory casserole with vegetables between layers of baked rice. The main course is called abgoosht. It started out as a stew of sorts, with beef, potatoes, veggies, tomatoes and spices. After cooking, we take the stock and serve it separately as a soup. The beef and vegetables are eaten separately. I hope you are enjoying, and yes, I do have some help in the kitchen," Kurt said.

When Alilah was close to finishing her meal, she started to gently probe the best way she could, "Kurt, I know next to nothing about you, your role in Iran, or who you represent. We have talked about lots of general ideas- invading Israel and the West but who are you, really? Obviously, you have funding; exactly who will we be working with? Tell me your beliefs," she said, "why have we been placed together; will we be setting up the next national or the next worldwide terrorist plot?"

"So many questions, Alilah. My answers might be beyond belief and my story will require you to forgo your knowledge and insights and re-imagine history Alilah. How well studied are you on the end of World War 2?" asked Kurt.

"Just as I've read in the history books, I guess," she said.

"The textbooks spell it out that way," Kurt responded, "but as you know, there are lots of details during and after war, which include the country you stand in right now."

"I was not aware that Iran had any involvement. Fill me in," Alilah said.

"Iran became the location of a third meeting among allied leaders. In 1943 Roosevelt, Churchill and Stalin met in Tehran. The meeting went on as planned, but several reports were made of an assassination attempt on all three leaders by German agents."

"What happened? I never heard of this? Did security catch these German agents?" she asked.

"No, the conference was completed," Kurt said, "Even before the war, Germany tried to influence Iranians, sending pro-Nazi books and even helped the Shah categorize Persians as 'pure blood Aryans', trying to convince Iranians of their kinship to Germans. And this was easy to do since the Reza Shah and Germany were allies as the war raged on."

"Did that work?" she asked.

"I can only guess," he said. "Prior to the war, and just after, about one thousand Germans immigrated to Iran and found jobs, mostly within government. Today, that number is about the same. As you can probably guess, I am partly of German descent. My mother was Persian."

"That is about all I did figure out Herr Huette!" said Alilah.

"I might look a little younger than my real age; I am 64, I have always taken care of myself, kept in shape and never have had to do any real manual labor. Our family has extreme wealth, and I have been well cared for," he said.

"I can see," Alilah said.

"But our family story goes beyond the wealth, and what I will tell you will shock you now. If I had taken my father's real name you would be speaking with Kurt Hitler," he said, "And that must remain our secret."

Alilah gasped, "Hitler, that cannot be possible!"

"This is also where the books have it all wrong. As my father desired, the Fourth Reich continues to develop strongly around the world as we speak, not only here and in Europe but in the United States as well. The beginning of the end of World War 2 was evident, and my father saw this coming before the landing of the troops in

Normandy. When he realized a storm had brewed and an allied invasion imminent, he launched a plan to escape, putting some of his highest-ranking men in charge of defense. He also ordered certain other friends in the military to escape to South America and to Africa on submarines. My father, on the other hand, took an overland route to Iran; he had placed many men in the Iran government in the years before and several thousand Germans lived in Iran. Thus, he knew he had friends in high places here and in other countries in the Middle East. Unfortunately, the landscape had changed a bit since his early interaction with the Arab countries and Iran," Kurt described. "My father died when I was 23, and I now am charged with completing his mission."

"Can I assume the mission has changed since the end of World War 2," Alilah asked.

"No, it has not. But I want to brief you on the history of Persia and Iran and the Jewish people. It may help in understanding our current situation. Over the last 2,500 years or so, the relationship between the Persians and Jewish people has fluctuated. Sometimes good, but mostly bad blood has existed between them. Several times in the history of this land, the Jews were exiled by different leaders, not just by Persians, but they kept coming back," Kurt continued, "In the 1900's, the history merges closer to our mission and our unified goals.

"Alilah, you might know this, but if not, the Muslim Brotherhood, founded in 1928, has its roots in Nazism. Its founder, Hassan al-Banna, based many of his teachings on my father's writings, including the eradication of all Jews."

"I knew his name but never knew he developed his teaching based on your father," said Alilah.

"In 1936, riots broke out under the command of al-Husseini, President of the Supreme Muslim Council. He recruited armed militias who attacked Jews. But even though the Jews were organized, British forces interceded to quell the uprising," said Kurt, "So, for many years, the Germans and Muslims had a common enemy."

"As I said, the mission has not changed, but tactics have changed. Early in the twentieth century, in the 1930s, Germany sent top leaders to Iran, providing University professors, its Scientific library, accountants, and even soldiers for training. Like I told you, Reza Shah and my father were close through 1943 when they attempted to kill the allied leaders. My father snuck into Iran just about that time. The German success was evident. Many Arab nations admired and sided with both my father and Heinrich Himmler, believing in total elimination of the Jewish population."

"So, the world has changed in so many ways since the end of the war and since the 1970s since your father died. What is the plan for the Fourth Reich, and how will it be organized in this mansion in the middle of nowhere Iran?" Alilah asked.

"You seem to have little confidence; as I said, we have spread our army all over the globe, even before the end of World War 2. As I said, my father knew the war was turning. When the U.S. entered the war after Japan bombed Pearl Harbor, it was only a matter of time before Roosevelt escalated his alliance with Churchill beyond his lend-lease program of providing arms to the UK. As U.S troops started to arrive by boatloads and increased by the hundreds of thousands by 1944, it was clear that my father had made the correct decision.

After Roosevelt and Churchill met in Morocco in early 1943, my father quietly left Germany in 1943. He read the stars and knew that these two powers, along with Stalin, would at this time block his plans, at least for now. He had one last hope, however, for this war and the Third Reich and continued to run the war from Iran. I told you about his one last hope. That also did not go as planned. When all three Allied leaders met in Iran, the attempted assassination never took place in Tehran. And, the war did end as you summarized above," he said.

"There must be much more to this since you and our sympathizers are scattered around the globe," Alilah said.

"Much more. To begin with, my father's top collaborators also went underground both before and right at the conclusion of the war. Egypt and Syria gave refuge to Nazi war criminals. Some of the Nazis, in due time, started to expose people to Nazi ideology. Today, the next generation is training Assad's senior intelligence officers in Nazi torture techniques. This fits into the spreading of Naziism in the Middle East. Many other top officers took U-boats to African nations and to South America.

After arriving, they settled into several countries, living clandestine everyday lives yet keeping the hope of a resurgence of a Fourth Reich. These were key leaders. Large numbers of people, 12 million, left Germany after the war, many were Nazis. They represented a good base whose next generations have multiplied and readied to be called upon. In the United States after the war, about 400,000 Germans came to the U.S. from 1946 to 1953, and the numbers kept rising. These Germans assimilated into the American way of life, but many kept their loyalty to the Nazi Party, as did their children. We call them crypto Nazis.

Even before the war, Charles Lindbergh and the Christian Front developed into a strong, sympathetic pro-Nazi group, remnants of which remain very effective in their antisemitic activities today. With time, as the political winds shifted in the States and the country became more divided in the latter part of the twentieth century, we began to see the timing ripening. Our internal

U.S. Nazi groups started to foment more right-wing movements, and slowly more right-wing groups developed and expanded. Our plans were made easier after Osama bin Laden led the attacks on the World Trade Center in 2001. This did not figure into our preparation but it did accelerate by many years our moves. Here the radical Muslims became our friends without their knowledge, which is why we are now linked again."

Kurt walked over to the bar to get a glass of cognac that he had poured out earlier. He cupped it in his hand for a minute, swirled it a bit, and took a big sniff. He continued to hold it for a minute or two while Alilah while watched him. Finally, he took a relatively large sip, seemed to move it around in his mouth for a bit and then swallowed.

"Okay, where were we? So, despite the appearance of just the two of us in one large mansion in Iran, a cohesive organization does exist worldwide. I have worked on plans and modified them for years. Now you have happened to join our group, and I know you can help," Kurt said.

"I don't know what skills I have. I don't add anything to whatever you could be planning," she said.

"For now, I need a companion, so to speak. I really need a woman who I can travel with and can pass as my wife. And this is the 21st century, Alilah. You are more than that. We are moving forward in many ways. You and I have the same ideals and goals," he said, "I have left Iran only a very few times, and when I did, I only journeyed to nearby nations. I have seen colleagues in Saudi Arabia and Kuwait a few times. Now is the time that we must meet our collaborators and discuss plans in detail; you will meet with them, a woman, as my equal in our plans."

"I can do that, and I read people pretty well. So, I can play my role with you in these plans and the overall picture. But I do not know the plans yet. You must tell me in advance the blueprints for the future and what we will be doing as we meet our collaborators," she asserted.

"Fair enough, if you're ready for more tonight,"

"I am not. I am tired, and I think it can wait until tomorrow. I have just absorbed a lot of information, much of which is almost unbelievable," Alilah said, "Let's pick it up tomorrow morning, OK."

"Fine with me. Good evening."

"Good night." Alilah said.

As Alilah headed up to her room, Kurt took a few steps over to the bar and poured himself a second glass of Hennessy XXO Cognac. Not only was he worth it, after reviewing all that of history with Alilah and thinking of upcoming plans, but he needed to calm down a little before heading off to sleep.

Kurt sat in his large leather chair, lit a cigar and sat back. First, he did feel pretty good for the first time in many years. He finally thought that the world had brought him a partner, someone with the brains and credentials that could help him in integrating his plans. But now he needed to speak all the truth to Alilah in the morning.

First, as he sipped his cognac, he thought to himself how he would speak to Alilah in the morning about several things. Alilah's presence was no accident. All the moves and arrangements made, starting with the Imam's passport and papers for "Sabina" from Baltimore and the tickets all the way to Iran, had been completed by Kurt's web in conjunction with Islamic extremists. He had ulterior motives as well. Kurt wanted to perpetuate the Hitler family lineage. Up to now, he had not married and found a suitable partner living in Iran. Alilah had the perfect spirit. Kurt was the product of an Aryan man and a Persian woman, so why shouldn't Alilah, an Iraqi woman, bear his children.

Kurt planned to work with Alilah in Iran and train with her for a year or two. If, after this time, he deemed her a proper leader of the organization, he also planned to make her commander-in-chief at some future date. At 64, he knew he needed a backup and hoped that Alilah would be that person.

At breakfast, the next morning, business continued.

"Our network remains very strong and our secrets tight in this wide world. Do you know why Alilah?" Kurt asked as Alilah came into the dining area off the expansive kitchen.

"Good morning, Kurt," she said, "Jumping right in, are you! Please let me grab a cup of coffee and some fruit and yogurt and then you can tell me all I do not know."

"Before I picked you up in Tehran, I had not communicated directly with anyone from outside Iran in several years. And our network has used very unsophisticated methods to keep in contact these last few years. I did not want a breakdown in any security or secrets that we passed around the globe. Our methods use individual messengers on camels, horses, bikes, cars, buses, ferries and any form of travel that do not or could not grab attention. It might take longer to get a word to our teams, but I avoid all electronic methods. We stay under any radar and away from any hackers. I see from all the news that even the world's top government war machines can be hacked. The United States Pentagon, the Chinese People's Liberation Army Command Center, and the Russian National Defense Management Center- they have all been hacked. Anyone, any country, can be broken. I maintain that old-school communication, although slow, maintains secrecy as long as we have trusted people in our network. Can I trust you, Alilah?"

"Kurt, you have brought me into your home. You obviously have strong ties to extremists and the radical Muslim group that I worked with, and the Imam who took me this far. You told me your family secret. You told me your communication method. You must trust me too," she said.

"I think I do. I can either trust you or kill you. Right now, I am sensing I trust you," he said, "You have told me much of what you have done in raising money but nothing in action."

"From my count, killing runs in the family," Alilah said with a wry smile, "So, that would be simple. How can I raise your level of trust in me?"

"First, I have yet to kill anyone, but certainly, I am very capable. As for trust, this will come in time as we work together and I see your performance."

Alilah stood up quickly and startled Kurt, but she only went to fill her coffee. They both had an uncomfortable laugh. Kurt relaxed after a moment, and they both sat back and finished their breakfast.

Kurt implied in his explanation to Alilah that he had wielded great power in many nations, including Saudi Arabia. He went on to explain to Alilah how the Saudi's developed a good relationship with America prior to 9/11 and the decades before. "Mostly because of oil," he said, "Oil in exchange for security. Some people thought it was only rumor, but after the attacks of 9/11, the very next day the CIA arranged for leading Saudi citizens to leave the U.S. despite an air ground stop in effect for days. And, Saudis continued to invest heavily in to US, lending billions of dollars, buying up real estate and many corporations in America."

"I know all this," said Alilah.

Kurt said, "But did you know that many of these investments were made at my own suggestion, through intermediaries. 9/11 started to derail the U.S. government's good relationship with Saudi Arabia. Osama bin Laden, the mastermind behind 9/11, was a Saudi. And, the United States itself became an exporter of oil."

"Iran, where I have been brought now is so much different." Alilah said, "Where we are sitting and speaking about history twenty years ago is a country unlike the times in 2001. Iran has enough enriched uranium to the point that it could make weapons-grade material within days. The U.S. knew this and unfortunately gave the country cash in the Obama years that might have helped fund this capacity."

"How does this impact us and our plans, Alilah?" asked Kurt, seemingly perturbed by her interrupting him.

"Since I do not know the plans yet, I cannot answer the question. But, if your, rather our, group does anything that disrupts Western and Mideastern stability, Iran will certainly see this as an opportunity to move in and use its influence and weapons," she said.

"Well, I am very pleased to be in the company of someone who thinks several moves ahead.

"One more thing," Alilah said, "As an outsider, I am not fooled by the small and younger, more liberal population in Iran that has gained worldwide attention and support from the West. We all recall when a young woman who refused to wear her hijab in public and was brutally beaten by the morality police and died. Many thousands were jailed for protesting a woman's death. At that time, the government superficially seemed to relax their concerns of the many women who began to stop wearing the hijab. The authoritarian Iranian Government, I am confident, has a close watch on any reform movements, and nothing of significance will come of it."

"Thank you for that insight. I just want you to know that I have played both sides, paying taxes to the government and supporting the reform movements."

Kurt told Alilah that he had stirred the pot with his underground influence in Iran for many years now. Kurt's compatriots around the globe under his command were always ready to carry out attacks, all of which appeared random. A hotel bombing in Bali, a drone crash into a commercial building in Los Angeles, a chemical spill on a New York subway car and many more against military and civilian targets. No particular patterns would stand out. In many cases, his people left fabricated evidence suggesting that Islamic Militants backed by Iran carried out the attacks.

"Here in Iran, you and I will then incite the "liberal" movement in order to keep the West and the government of Iran off guard. The United States will lose focus on Iran, keeping primary watch on other targets. Iran will lose its focus as well. We can build a power base right here under the distracted eyes of the Iranian government. I already have connections to many underground leaders. They do not plan to ally themselves with the West or other liberals. Their interest lies only in the money I provide them. They are my mercenary protestors," Kurt said.

Alilah liked Kurt's planning and began to feel more comfortable with him.

She could now almost envision an advance of power around the world right from his home. She grew more excited thinking about the possibilities. Alilah knew he had waited years to see the slow accumulation of tactical assets. No one expected or knew of his powerful underground army, as his invisible colleagues grew in numbers from the 1980s to the present tremendous numbers around the globe, especially in the United States.

"So, why me? Why did you take me to the center of your group?" asked Alilah.

"You have connections we need in the United States and Western Europe. And now, after two years in Iran, it was time for us to move out together," he said.

"To where?"

"As leader of the Fourth Reich, I have been sequestered in Iran for most of his life. I must go out and see my generals. But first, you and I will visit the Middle East and Asia, avoiding the watchful eye of border patrol agents," Kurt said, "I own a large yacht on the Persian Gulf, in the Port of Bushehr. I use it infrequently but it is ready to go and can to a speed of over forty knots. You and I will board this ship and be in Saudi Arabia in less than half a day. Are you ready."

"I have been ready for action for a long time," Alilah said, smiling for the first time in what seemed like years.

8

Gone For Good

August 2019

"Don't cry, Najah, Mommy will come home, and Papi is getting us more ice cream tomorrow," said Aamir, her twin brother.

"I don't want ice cream. I want Mommy. She said she would be back in three days. Where is she?" Najah said weeping

Aamir didn't answer and didn't know any better as a seven-year-old. He tried to make his sister and best friend feel better every day, as best he could. He also thought about his mom all the time and about going home to Baltimore to see his friends and their father. This was summer break. The promise of ice cream at the beach didn't mean much to them anymore. Now, after a week had passed, she had not called, and Jidi and Papi had no answers. Aamir could hear his grandparents, Jidi and Papi, cry sometimes as well.

Despite the crying, Aamir saw that his grandparents put on a great show every day. This morning, the breakfast table in the kitchen had plenty of choices for the kids. All the sugar-filled and not-so-nutritious cereals advertised on the cartoon shows, as well as fresh fruit to go with them, were ready for them on the table. The kids filled their bowls to the top and ate most of the contents.

"Papi, why were those strange men here a few days ago asking questions about Mommy and Daddy," asked Aamir as he and Najah finished their cereal and began to drink their orange juice.

"Aamir, your father is a brilliant scientist. They need to ask him some questions about a new virus outbreak and cannot seem to locate him. They wanted to see if we knew where he or your mother were traveling," said Papi, making up a story that the child could believe, "I told them I did not know for sure where they were."

"Okay," he said.

And just like that, in a matter of minutes, Aamir sensed a change in Papi as he glanced out the window. What started as a fairly typical morning became interrupted when a large black Ford SUV arrived at the front of the Farooq home. Two nicely dressed men, both about six feet tall in dark grey suits, exited their SUV and walked to the front door. Aamir noticed they were the same men who had asked about Mommy and Daddy. Papi met them before they could ring the bell. Aamir and Najah finished their breakfast and scampered up the stairs to their bedroom.

"Good morning, gentlemen," said Papi. "How can I help you today?"

"Good morning, Mr. Farooq. As you may recall, I am Jack Adams, and this is Matthew McDonald." Jack said, "We would like to speak with you and your wife once again about your daughter, if you don't mind."

"Please come in, and we want to speak with you also. Maybe you have information on Sabina," said Papi.

"Nice to see you again, but the news we have may not be pleasant," said McDonald.

"Oh, no! Please don't tell me she's hurt," Johara cried.

"No, nothing like that. I am sorry for Mr. McDonald's phrasing," said Jack.

"Would you like some tea before we start," asked Johara.

"No, thank you. That is very kind. Let us just ask a few questions, and I think we can leave you alone for the rest of the day," said Jack.

"When did you last see your daughter Sabina," asked McDonald bluntly.

"She arrived here last Friday, late morning, more or less. I don't exactly remember the time," Johara said meekly.

"Can you be more specific?" McDonald said.

"Let me take this from here," said Jack, "We hope to get a better idea of when Sabina arrived and when she might have left your home. Then we can track her other movements either in the country or if she left the United States."

"Oh, I understand," said Fadi, "Sabina arrived in a car, not her own, but someone dropped her and her children off around 11 in the morning on Friday. She said she had car trouble in Rhode Island and took a ride here. She had last-minute plans to visit an old friend in Paris for the weekend. This friend, I do not remember her name, do you Johara?"

"Yes, Alice Germaine," said Johara.

"Yes, that's it. OK," said Fadi, "So, of course, we could not wait to have the grandkids for a few days. Sabina planned to be in Paris for the weekend and return on Monday. We have not spent too much time with the children, and since school was out for summer, there was no rush in returning them back to Baltimore."

"I understand. Sabina arrives late morning in an Uber or some other vehicle and spends a few hours with you, correct?" asked Jack.

"Yes. She seemed fine, just a little anxious to leave to see her friend," said Johara.

"I agree," said Fadi.

"Did she act like this on all her visits?" asked McDonald.

"As I said, she did not visit that often," Fadi said.

Clearly, Matthew McDonald's occasional questioning during the interview irritated the Farooq's. Something about his questions just was not smooth or hit tender spots. Or he may have been less experienced or just wanted answers quickly and to get out of there. McDonald was not on his game today.

Jack took over again, "Do you have any information on the flight she was on?"

"We do not know the flight, but she hurried out of here, so I think it was probably a late afternoon or early evening flight." Farooq said, "She wanted to stay the whole weekend with her friend Alice and then leave late on Sunday and come back early on Monday, arriving Monday midday."

"I have a few more questions, and we will be finished; we apologize for taking up your time," Jack said.

"No, no of course not. We want to know what has happened to Sabina. She is a good girl. Alan must have her mixed up in something bad…please find her," said Fadi, "Come back if you have to ask more questions."

"I have a few tough questions for you, Fadi and Johara: Well, do you think she really went to Paris? Or somewhere else in the States? If she did nothing wrong with her husband, why did she leave this weekend?" asked Jack, "I know these are difficult questions, and you might have to think about the answers and call me back."

"I cannot believe she was involved with these horrible attacks we saw on the news last night. I think her traveling to see us and then on to her friend in Paris is just a coincidence," said Fadi, "So that is my answer. I do not think she would have left if she knew the trouble Alan got himself into."

"I agree. I have nothing more to say. I need to take care of my grandchildren now, who I hope have not heard any of this. They are very smart." said Johara. Feeling weak, she took several quick breaths she settled into a chair in the living room.

"Well, thank you both for your time. We plan to interview the Imam in Baltimore. If he tells us anything important, we will keep you informed. Also, if your grandchildren say anything to you that might help us, let me know. Sometimes, they can be like sponges and pick up all kinds of information we do not hear or see. We hope we did not disturb your day, but I think we both want the same thing, to find Sabina and make sure she is safe," said Jack.

With that, the two men left through the front door. Aamir and Najah had been upstairs playing but knew something unusual had been happening. Aamir watched the front lawn, and when they entered into their car, he ran to the staircase.

"Those were the same men who asked about Mommy and Daddy before, right?" said Aamir, with Najah from the staircase. All Jidi could do was cover her face as tears ran down her cheek.

"Everything will be alright," Papi lied again, "Please, there is nothing to worry about."

Aamir believed his grandfather, but as the days had gone by, even for a child, he began to sense a problem.

That night, Aamir could not console Najah. Jidi could hear whimpering from the upstairs bedrooms. She took to the stairwell and went up to the second floor as fast as her weary body would take her. In the front bedroom of the three-bedroom home, Najah lay under her covers crying. Jidi slowly pulled the covers back and saw that Najah's eyes were reddened and her face so very wet with tears.

She struggled to get out the words, "I want Mommy back."

Jidi said, "We want her back here too, angel, and we are trying to find her."

Najah half sat up and hugged Jidi. Najah's pajama top, wet with tears, needed changing.

"We are supposed to be back home. I want to go home with Mommy and Aamir."

"Okay, let's see what tomorrow brings; you need to go to sleep, angel; it is late. Let me get you a dry shirt and read you a book. Okay?" said Jidi.

"Okay, I love you," said Najah, and they kissed each other.

9

Getting Into Battles
December 2021

Kurt's mood rose to a high he had not felt for many months since he brought Alilah into his fold. He took the wheel of his Toyota Land Cruiser and they began the overland trip to the south of Iran. He felt elated to be leaving the country after several years. He knew this was the time to get on the road with his partner and evaluate the tactics he had been working on over the years. After they drove for hours and arrived at the port, the sun began to set, not allowing time to get out to sea that day. The ship, docked, stocked and ready for the next day, was ready for boarding, and the crew was prepared.

As Alilah and Kurt boarded, he took a cursory view of the deck and waved to the first mate on board. He and Alilah went below to a sitting area outside the bedrooms, where the server awaited. She asked if they would like a late supper. They both were famished.

"Could you bring us some fresh fish that the chef might have, if that is alright with you, Alilah?" Kurt asked.

"That sounds delightful. I really am hungry. A loaf a bread would be great also," she said.

"I will get on it right away," said the server, "My name is Renee; just ring my bell any time you need me."

"Renee, before you walk away, could you bring us two champagne flutes," Kurt asked.

"Of course, sir," she said with a smile.

Kurt walked to the yacht's wine refrigerator and pulled out a bottle of champagne. He popped a bottle of Krug Grand Cuvee Brut, the best he had in stock, and poured two tall glasses. Why not the best, he thought, he did feel close to Alilah now, after almost two years together, and they were embarking on an important mission.

"Alilah, it is time to celebrate the beginning of our adventure and the start of our new world. We have just begun. Let us drink to our future success and hope someday that the dreams of my father and your people come to a realization. To the future," he toasted, and they both drank their full flutes.

Kurt refilled them. The server appeared with a plate of cheeses, vegetables, pita, and hummus, as well as slices of bread.

"I hope this holds you over for a few more minutes," Renee said, and she walked out briskly.

"Yes, thank you very much," said Alilah.

Alilah could not wait. She grabbed a pita and pushed it down into the bottom of the hummus bowl, taking a huge gob in order to immediately satiate her appetite. Kurt almost fell off his chair, laughing. It might have been her action or the fact that he had downed his second glass of champagne having not eaten anything for hours. It should have been a light moment for the both of them, but it did not turn out as such.

Alilah, not too pleased with his behavior, said, "Well if you aren't hungry, go ahead, sit there and drink some more. You just made a beautiful toast, and I thought this would be the start of a 'new world tour'. I thought we could act like normal people around each other. Are we not a little closer after all this time. I think you also should get something in your belly, then we can talk about our plans for the week and years ahead."

"You are absolutely right. I am sorry. Let me have some of that food before I make any more stupid actions," he said. Kurt took some cheese and bread and also filled his glass for a third time.

"Thank you, Kurt. Now, just sip that one, okay," she said.

"Yes, dear," Kurt replied, with some sarcasm. This certainly did not go well with Alilah.

"I mean it, please, you really do not seem to be holding your alcohol, and you have not had much this evening," she said.

"I will tone it down. I am sorry," he said, "We have a job to do, and we will dine and talk shortly." And with that they sat in silence for the next several minutes as Alilah had another glass of champagne herself.

Moments later, dinner came out, and it looked delicious. Alilah waited for Kurt to take the first bite, only so she would not hear any more laughing. Of course, none was heard. A wonderful bottle of Les Monts Damnés sancerre was also brought to the table, and that paired well with the fresh black streaked monocle bream sautéed with fresh vegetables. The fabulous dinner eaten too quickly by both of them, did not last long as they were so hungry. It was so much better than anything Kurt, Alilah or his staff had prepared in his home. Fresh fish right off the water certainly could not be beaten. Coffee and some pastries completed the menu, but Kurt insisted on finishing off the evening with a tumbler of XO Remy Martin Cognac. It was quite good and topped off the delicious meal.

The champagne, wine and cognac did have quite an effect on Alilah, more so than on Kurt, who, before dinner, was probably more obnoxious than tipsy from just two glasses of champagne. She did not abide by strict Muslim religious beliefs, in which alcohol is considered haram or forbidden. She partook in alcohol ever since she had left home as a teen. She had learned from some of her friends that drinking alcohol was morally acceptable. The yacht had three staterooms, and Alilah went to her own on the far left of the ship. Kurt moved toward his stateroom, the larger room in the center of the yacht.

"Good night, Alilah. Most likely, we will be on our way before we awake in the morning. The trip should take about 6 to 7 hours as the captain mapped it out," he said, "And it should be smooth. If we are lucky, we might see a whale or two also."

"I look forward to a restful sleep and a day at sea and maybe some whale watching. If I eat like that again, there might be a whale close by. I had a nice dinner after our appetizers…. no, really, I enjoyed our time tonight, and I think after such a long time we are starting to understand each other. Goodnight, Kurt," and she turned to her room.

Alilah did not rest and could not sleep. So many thoughts drummed through her head. She could not tell if she felt the excitement looming for the coming days and weeks ahead or if the alcohol had changed her dreary mood of months past. Alilah always acted as if nothing bothered her. She realized she had a strong character and cared for her children, parents and previous job. But her marriage had been a lost cause.

Her husband only focused on developing biological weapons of mass destruction, and for years, he never showed any love for her. And now, after more than two years, seeing what was ahead, all her energy was tapped, and tears poured out of her eyes. She could not hold them back any longer. The stress of the training had finally gotten to her. The physical and mental drills she had endured for months on end became exhausting. The discussion of the long-term planning for the next one to two years and beyond became anguishing. Kurt had implied eventually she would assume a leading world role. He would be in his seventies in less than ten years and needed new leadership, envisioning Alilah in that highest role. He may have implied other things about the future between them, but she was not sure.

It didn't take a genius to understand that Kurt had no wife or children for the next generation 'Hitler'. Could I fit the role she imagined? In any case she realized now she was ready for action - not further planning. She was hopeful that this trip was the beginning of operations. If not, she thought to herself, this might not be her team. But on the other hand, she now felt that she had worked with Kurt far too long and started to have feelings for him, why give up on his plans now? These thoughts twisted in her head as her body tossed and turned for a long time. She continued to stare out the port hole at the lights on the dock.

Another hour later, she knocked on Kurt's door. He had been asleep and awoke with a start, always on alert. He slowly opened his door and saw her standing at the door. She walked right in and hugged him very briefly. In the almost two years that they had worked together, they had very little physical contact, so this surprised Kurt. She walked to the corner of his room and sat on a large sofa; he followed and sat next to her.

"What is wrong Alilah? It is very late. I do not mind you waking me, but tell me, what is bothering you?" he pleaded.

"I do not know," she lied.

"You must. You have never come to me in the middle of the night in two years with any issues. Is it the strange surroundings?" he asked.

"No, I do not know what we are doing here. Yes, you tell me, and we go over and over and over all the big plans and the years it will take to 'run the world,' but do I want to run the world? No, I just want justice for the innocent Muslims that have been killed and Arabs who have been pushed off their lands," Alilah said, almost in tears.

"May I take your hand," Kurt said softly.

"Yes," said Alilah.

Kurt held her hand and tried to relieve some of the tension she felt.

"Alilah, we will fight for justice," Kurt rubbed her shoulder as she calmed down a little more, "Together, in time, we will attack on many fronts and take control as we planned. Do not be impatient."

"I will try not to be."

"Alilah, I know you must have many feelings right now. I do too," said Kurt, "We have been working very closely together for a long time. I must tell you I have strong feelings for you that I have not shared. Now I will"

"I have feelings for you as well," said Alilah, starting to breathe rapidly but feeling much better than before.

"Alilah, you are beautiful and intelligent, and we both seem to want the same things in life. I must admit I am older than you, but I would like to be with you," said Kurt.

Alilah took Kurt's hand, and they went to his bed. Sitting down, Alilah took his pajama top off over his head without undoing the three buttons.

"Are we sure we want to do this? It will change our whole relationship," Kurt said.

"No, I am not sure." She lay down on the bed, waiting. He curled down beside her and squeezed so tightly she could barely catch her breath.

They made love again in the morning.

She felt much better than she had before she came to his cabin. In two years, this was the first time she had been physically close to a man. If the relationship would change, so be it. She heard the boat pull out, and they were off to Saudi Arabia. Now, Alilah thought that the world conquest might be a lot sweeter for both of them.

"I think our travels together might be more exciting, Kurt," Alilah whispered in his ear as they rested on the bed.

"We will make some time for work, but you my dear, might get in the way," he said as he turned her over and massaged her back lightly.

After showering and dressing in the morning in their own cabins, the two of them met in the sitting area outside the cabins and called for a light breakfast and coffee. A moderate chop was expected on the seas the whole trip to Saudi Arabia and Kurt was hoping Alilah would handle the trip without any problem. Breakfast arrived in just a few minutes. Renee set out plates of cheeses, hard-boiled eggs, salmon, bread, and coffee. She provided nothing too heavy to start the day, given the weather and possible rough seas ahead.

Following breakfast, Alilah's excitement of being on a huge private vessel could not be contained. She wanted to go right up to the sun deck, even though it was none too sunny. Kurt and Alilah took the stairs up three decks to the top of the ship and looked out on the water. Not much to see but Alilah hoped to get a view of at least one whale or other marine life. She scanned the waters, port and starboard. And she kept looking all over, as these seas were known for humpbacks and an occasional orca.

It did not take but a few minutes for her to start to feel a little queasy and then nauseated. Kurt suggested that she not move her head so much and not scan the waters, just look at one place, a point on the horizon. This advice did not help. She felt cold and clammy, and then went to her cabin for the next five hours. Kurt checked on her every hour or so. She did not get any worse but was not ready to get on deck until landing in Saudi Arabia.

The captain knew not to dock at a small port in the northern part of Saudi Arabia on the Persian Gulf. It might have been closer in his sea route but not worth the risk. Facial recognition was used in passport control areas in all the ports, but Kurt had contacts at the port near the city of Dammam at the giant King Abdul Aziz Sea Port. Kurt's men in the country had connections with the port authority, and this made for easy entry for anybody who wanted entry into the country. They "took care" of the connections, thanks to Kurt's bankroll.

The captain took the yacht a little further south and pulled into this huge port, which in years past was a largely commercial fishing town until oil became the currency of Saudi Arabia. Now a huge port, one could see almost nothing but commercial oil tankers in all the piers. The trip to this port took about 40 minutes longer, but Kurt always preferred entering this town the few times he himself went to Saudi Arabia. Furthermore, the road to Riyadh connected directly to the port city.

From the eastern Gulf Port town of Dammam, Kurt and Alilah would take an overland route with a Saudi driver to Riyadh. Their next stop on their mission did not come close to resembling hand-to-hand combat or biological warfare.

Before docking Kurt had one of the crew call a friend who drove to meet their driver. The contact told the driver where to meet Kurt and Alilah. There would never be any direct contact between Kurt and anyone on land. The ship's captain took all the passports and cash and brought them to the "correct" officials at the immigration office. Within a matter of minutes, all documents were stamped, and all crew and passengers were cleared to disembark.

His pick-up would be off the town center. After about a one-kilometer sweltering walk from the port entry, passing multiple bait shops, restaurants, markets, a pharmacy, as well as an antique shop, they finally arrived. Just beyond the grass circle in the old town center, they spotted the Toyota Land Rover. The car was running and cooled to a very comfortable temperature. They approached the vehicle, entered the back seat and said hello to Ishmael, the name confirmed by the crewman. The air conditioning was on full blast. The only thing Kurt did was confirm the destination.

"So," said Kurt, leaning over to Alilah when they got into the back of the second Land Rover of the trip. "Do you like computer games?"

She looked at him strangely. She knew that video gaming development was now a huge economic growth area in Saudi Arabia. Kurt moved closer to her and told her that he and his band of worldwide terrorists had recently recruited the top company working on a popular game. This group just happened to be associated with a mosque in Saudi Arabia raising funds for Kurt's work. As an upgrade for a very popular militaristic game, a programmer embedded many 'interesting' touches into his game.

These changes, which only expert players would find, expressed extreme racist, homophobic and antisemitic messages. The messages suggested that action be taken against those persons if you thought they wronged you or someone close to you. Once an expert found these hidden notes, they could be shared with less proficient gamers. No one in the quality department would ever find these deeply embedded program changes, but enough players would, and they would disseminate the directives. Soon directives and challenges spread around the world as the popular game hit the top of the charts.

"Who are we going to see?' she asked.

"A game programmer at a company called Gammozunk. We need to take gaming to the next level of propaganda and spread it on a grander scale." They both laughed at the name.

"So, Kurt we need to go this Gammo something or other now," said Alilah.

"That's the plan," he said, "We need to get our programmer to move the game to the next level, spread it on a grander scale, and hopefully make it easier to access."

Alilah could not believe where this company was located. On the drive into Riyadh, nothing but beautiful architecture could be seen; this place was a mess from the outside. They pulled onto a nondescript side street and went to the second floor of a walk-up building. Several modern tech companies were housed in this complex incubator facility, including a company named Gammozunk.

As soon as they arrived, a young man came out dressed in a modern suit. Kurt whispered to Alilah, "I feel like he's the young son and apprentice I have never had!"

"Let's hope so," said Alilah.

"Good afternoon, I am Kurt Huette, and this is my associate, Alilah Cetin," said Kurt.

"Hello, I am Shareef Akil. It is nice to meet you, and I must say it is unusual for me to entertain visitors here at Gammozunk," he replied.

"Well, I hope we are not intruding, but we are fascinated with the game you developed called Mean Man Hunt, at least that is how it translates in English," Kurt said, "I have gotten into several deep levels of the game and really enjoyed the messages you have in the system."

"Thank you very much. That is very kind," said Shareef.

Shareef led them into a research and development area where huge screens on the wall could monitor ongoing gaming. Others were at computers in their cubicles, developing improvements on this one specific game.

"Shareef, I am glad you brought us here. We wish to speak to you about upgrading Mean Man Hunt," said Alilah.

"Improvements and correcting coding errors are one thing; upgrades are another and cost in terms of manpower and money," said Shareef."

"Well, we can handle that, and we want to speak about the reason for the upgrades," said Alilah.

"Yes, we know you have a similar interest as we do in global Intifada," said Kurt.

"Yes, but how do you know?" said Shareef.

"Let us not worry. We are on the same page, and your game can help us," said Alilah, "We want to use your game to recruit like-minded people to carry out our war. But we only want the best of the best.

"Yes, if they can complete tasks in the game, then they will be selected to participate in real-life deployment skills," said Kurt, "All of these persons will be videotaped, and only those with the best records will be chosen."

"All the chosen will be entered in the NNA, the Neo-Nazi Army. They have similar goals as we Muslims have," said Alilah, "Broader goals, but nonetheless, goals that overlap with ours.

"And the money, for the game and payouts, everything must be approved above me," said Shareef.

"I have already discussed this with your Board of Directors, Shareef. Do not despair," Kurt said, "Now is your time to move on this great project you have created. Your Board is very happy with you. Just make the 'Winners Circle' easier to attain; this should help us reach some more mature individuals also, not just the current 'gamers'. We need to think about making it more real. And do not worry, we will weed out those that do not deserve to work with us."

The remainder of the meeting did not last long. The three of them said their farewells, and Kurt and Alilah began their exit.

"That went well," Alilah said to him.

Kurt nodded. "It's going to get better. If Gammozunk's Mean Man Hunt worked as expected, then racism, antisemitism and all matters of hatred will escalate worldwide in the coming months. Our field generals need to be ready to control the ensuing war and subsequently take ground control of areas when prudent. Our main targets, the United States, France, Italy, Spain and southeast Asia, seem ready for exploitation. All have been primed by poor leadership, ongoing wars or our very well-placed propaganda machines."

Meanwhile, even before the games began and his troops grew, Alilah and Kurt received promising intelligence. The Neo-Nazi Army, his NNA, had made great strides, using their planned violence and scare tactics. Operating as a secret society now emboldened, they performed many tasks necessary to begin the quest to take over the country, one State at a time. Their missions amounted to seemingly trivial tactics, but Kurt knew they would start to mount up and become more than a nuisance. Pulling over a car without authority, petty thievery, and disrupting local events, all of which disturbed the public. With the mass shootings that had occurred, the general population began to isolate themselves and spend less time in public.

The NNA men and women carrying weapons and acting out around town made it even more difficult for ordinary people to go out and enjoy life. At Kurt's suggestion, many NNA members boldly wore swastikas in public and acted like they had authority. Many parents, afraid of influences on their children, began home-schooling their children. The NNA men and women did not appear organized, but of course, Kurt and Alilah knew better. Behind the scenes, their buttons were pushed, motivated by bias and hate.

And then, the verified videos from Mean Man Hunt started to pour in. The rewards for the crimes grew as the evil behaviors became more daring. Before long, Kurt's pool of persons from which to choose his top lieutenants multiplied. These anonymous potential NNA members were all paid through concealed cryptocurrency accounts, grew in the next three to six months, largely due to Gammozunk's worldwide market. Opportunities for expanding the NNA army existed not just in the United States but throughout the world. The NNA growth looked unstoppable.

10

Attacks On The Homeland

June 2021

Nari Lee read and studied the reports of killings, crashes and shootings during the summer and felt foolish. She imagined herself as a bright person. She did have two doctoral degrees, one in immunology and one in pharmaceutical sciences. And, on top of that, she's thinking, I am a trained CIA agent. She accepted she was not working on any of these cases, but come on, I should be able to put something together. Granted this was not laboratory data, but the same analyses applied.

Nari pulled together more information from police reports and more news stories. It began with a few wild rides and disastrous crashes into crowded fairs and farmer's markets on brilliant sunny Saturday afternoons. Unsuspecting people by the hundreds in small towns U.S.A. were killed or severely injured. These events did not happen all at once or all in one week. The crashes and now shootings in sold-out rock concerts from persons perched upon buildings 200 meters away occurred two and three weeks apart. Slowly, they started to happen with more regularity. A full-out investigation of the events was not even possible as so many occurred.

She saw that the killings kept on coming every week, brought to the country live from the street by reporters. Random reports like these continued for the last one to two years. Teens with guns ran in the streets, breaking up legitimate celebrations that appeared to be just for their amusement. But now, the killing spread like an uncontrolled burn throughout many states. Suddenly, the violent shooting deaths were not restricted to the inner cities. In Illinois, shootings fanned out from the South Side of Chicago to the north suburbs, to Rockford to the west of the city in the farmlands, south in Urbana, Springfield and even as far as Carbondale. These areas had not been known for the high levels of crime that the streets of Chicago had endured. Over the last six months, five seemingly random events struck down many innocent people.

A homicide bomber took out fifteen adults and children at a street fair in Springfield just two miles from the State Fairgrounds. Only a week after that, a young man in Rockford shot up a grocery store for no apparent reason. He may not have liked the produce. He started in those aisles and ended in the fish department, then pulled a gun and shot himself in the mouth. All in all, ten people were killed and three wounded seriously. In Carbondale, a teen driver, seemingly maddened by something, drove into the large farmer's market on Main Street and wounded twenty with no fatalities.

The Governor of Illinois called up the National Guard as a deterrent for the many problems occurring mostly on weekends around the State of Illinois. The commander of the Guard did his best to round up the required troops. Many of the Guard personnel did not show up for their required duty assignments. Some called in to ask for medical leave, others went to their post to see the medical staff, indicating they were not fit for duty. They felt their action in the field would be a suicide mission. The media called for an all-out halting of large events and gatherings in public places, such as done during the Covid pandemic. Nari hypothesized that hatred or misguided upbringing caused these mass shootings and killings but, for now, had no way to prove it.

Nari also observed other similar events that happened elsewhere. Right next door in the State of Iowa, a spate of similar incidents occurred, again with no explanation. But events like these were not confined to the middle of America. Maine, Connecticut, upstate New York, Nevada, Washington State, Florida, and many more areas all dealt with comparable emergencies. Nari found no connections between the persons involved and the actual tragedies that they started.

News of other tragedies came in beyond the United States. Similar bombings, shootings, fires, and large-scale 'accidents' occurred in Germany, Italy and France. The U.K saw its share as well, but very few involved shootings.

Nari found that perpetrators were alive in several cases at the scenes, but as she delved further into their backgrounds, nothing resembled a large-scale scheme or plot. This result frustrated the investigative teams directly working on the case. The living persons actually carrying out these attacks swore they had no forethought of their actions. According to the police Nari spoke with and reports she read, these people just collected what they needed and carried out their actions at the last minute. After the fact the accused had no idea why they committed these horrible attacks. Some interrogators thought that these individuals could have been placed under hypnotic suggestion.

Nari began to see other disturbing events happening with increased frequency across the nation as well. These phenomena were not person-on-person attacks but self-inflicted injuries. Observations, mostly in older high school students and even some college students, began to raise more alarm across the country. She noted that the CDC and others began to report large increases in eating disorders mostly in young women, but certainly not restricted to females. Kids without any prior history of anxiety developed anorexia.

Therapists and physicians, overwhelmed with all the new diagnoses on high school and college campuses in cities around the country, had no idea what hit this demographic. On the college campuses, eating problems had nothing to do with a student's inability to obtain food, even though some students may have only had two meals per day on their meal plans. Most schools had plenty of other options like fast foods and inexpensive snack foods available in student centers. In the home setting, there were no excuses for lack of eating. The CDC labeled the new disorder and called it "ETAAN, Epidemic teenage anorexia nervosa," with their best guess incidence of 2-3/1,000 individuals at risk in the age group 16 to 22.

Unfortunately, Nari found other even more disturbing information: a huge increase in teenage suicide. Over the last two years the rate just shot up. Suicides had increased in general, especially in middle-aged men, but now the young people of America and Europe had started to take their own lives. These victims, at their own hands, were particularly violent. Young women and men jumped off bridges at peak traffic hours, shot themselves in the head in public places, and dove off buildings onto streets below. No one really understood these public displays of violent self-destruction. As with those who suffered from anorexia, Nari could find no common factors among the suicide victims.

11

More Attacks - Foreign Or Domestic

July 2021

Having been briefed by their agents and underlings, CIA Director Martin Erlich and FBI Director Jonas Hamilton needed to meet in person. Each Agency had its own take on intelligence and it became necessary for leaders to synthesize the information brought to them. In the past, lack of communication between the agencies might just have been the cause of America losing a huge battle against al-Qaeda, the loss of the Twin Towers and the assault on the Pentagon on 9/11. These two men vowed not to let it ever happen when they had these positions. Ego would not stand in their way.

"We do not know for certain he has done anything. His reading material gives no hint," said Martin Erlich, "But Alan Mazer could have set something in motion before the other attacks; call it a living time bomb."

"How did you come up with that idea? How could Mazer pull off such an attack? He sits in a Federal Prison, with no contact with anyone except a phone call once in a great while. These are all monitored, and those calls have all been to his lawyers. No family, scientists, activists or other persons have contacted Mazer," said

Jonas Hamilton, "Yes, he reads scientific literature which we screen, but he cannot perform any experiments. He is locked down for life, just like all the other prisoners here. He is here for thirty life terms."

"Remember, not all viruses cause effects right away. Take HIV. You might get infected, but if not treated for the virus, symptoms could take a few years to develop," said Erlich, "Is it possible he put something like that out there? Nari Lee has my ears again."

"Isn't that a lot of conjecture?" asked Hamilton again.

As he questioned him, Erlich started thinking about the Imam in Baltimore. The Task Force never found much information or money in that mosque, but Sabina Mazer worked there for several years. She could have connections all over the world but the CIA or the Joint Task Force never connected her to these groups. Then Erlich was stopped in mid-thought…

"Hey Martin, you were just staring into space. What are you thinking?" said Hamilton.

"I thought the Imam in Baltimore did not give us much information. Yet, all this went down in the Virginia-Maryland area, including the highway bombings several years before. I figure that mosque might have a role, especially since Sabina, Mazer's wife, worked there for many years," said Erlich.

"So, we need to investigate again. But this does not relate to another virus, does it?""

"It may not but I suggest we put Dr. Nari Lee on this part of the case. First, she understands the virus pieces of this, and I could add her to join the JTTF from the CIA. That way, we are not stumbling over each other. That will give her more freedom on paper to operate within the States," said Erlich, "But you know as well as I do, we can still send her off on her own. This is a national security issue. CIA agents can certainly operate domestically."

"That's fine with me. Let's partner up Nari with someone else on the JTTF, a veteran FBI agent who might help in questioning. Jack Adams has actually interviewed the Farooq's twice before, just briefly. He indicated that more should be done. I think he could work well with Nari," said Hamilton.

"We will see about that. I just want her on the case now. We should question Mazer again soon," said Erlich, "His wife remains unaccounted for and could be planning another attack right now. He claimed he has no idea of her whereabouts, but a new virus he might have developed is a different subject altogether."

"We cannot question Sabina Mazer; we cannot find her. But Mazer could be questioned. We will have to speak to the Attorney General," said Hamilton.

12

A New Day in America - President Julia Moreno

January 2021

" . . . **I** will not continue much further with my address today. It is too cold out here. Our country has survived two hundred fifty years of wars, economic upheaval, civil unrest, large-scale disagreements and splits among our citizenry. But in between those times, we have built a great nation, one that the world looks to as a leader, one that at all times supports those in need around the globe. Now, we have gotten past the big divide. We can't go back. The people across this great nation have agreed. A woman can be the president of the United States of America and I will do my utmost best to prove that those that voted for me made the right choice. I make no claim to be the next George Washington, Abraham Lincoln, or John F Kennedy. We have had our share of good and not-so-good presidents. I only promise what I said when I took my oath of office just moments ago …to uphold the Constitution and duly defend the laws of our Nation and our People. I will not blame any person or prior administration for what I am dealt with as I take my office today. I will take on the issues head-on and work with Congress to fix problems and take on new challenges. What I do promise is a fair review of all legislation that hits my desk. I will only sign into law justifiable legislation and orders."

My fellow Americans let's be honest, we have many new people that have arrived across our borders. Many have come legally, many others illegally. Some of you might look at me with disdain because of my heritage. Let me tell you. I am a natural-born citizen of the United States of America. My parents worked hard to educate me. I did pretty well with their help. I represented the people of Florida in the House. And when I moved to New York I won a Senate seat. And now, as your leader, I will work just as hard to ensure everyone who is not a criminal stay in this country and raise their children in the land of the free. I look forward to leading you all as we approach new challenges in the 21st century. We have economic and employment issues to deal with, as I said. And so, my fellow Americans, we will work together on these and all the other issues. With your help in four years, we will look back and see that we have made excellent choices and great advances. God Bless You, and God Bless the United States of America. Thank You."

As President Julia Moreno finished her inaugural speech on this cold January morning, she took the arm of her husband and they both waved excitedly to the crowd. Cheers rose up and were deafening. The crowd had spanned every square foot from the Capitol Building to the Lincoln Memorial over two miles away. Large monitors had been placed approximately every one hundred yards. On this winter morning, all those attending had the unique chance to see the first woman president sworn in and speak to the nation, both those in the freezing cold and most of America and the world watching remotely. It had been a new day and the beginning of a new era for America.

13

Congressional Testimony

August 2021

11 AM FDA Presentation Concludes

Dr. Fredericka Lansing, Director, Center for Biologics Evaluation and Research (CBER)

Dr. Lansing, a middle-aged lean woman with long, flowing white hair, finished her hour-long presentation to the Congressional Committee investigating the disaster of the MVoneshot measles virus vaccine. This physician knew the vaccine really had not been needed, but it did provide one big advantage: a single dose gave lifelong immunity to the measles virus. That meant eventually, combined with other similar childhood vaccines, fewer injections for little kids would be needed. But a terrorist caused a disaster. A bright U.S. doctor, a jihadist, working with a source in the Company, switched the approved vaccine with a slightly different strain that was a killer. That strain caused infection of the brain and paralysis. Many children died or were maimed, really through no fault of the Company. Dr. Lansing now thought to herself that procedures really needed changing. The country was up in arms. Because of this unmitigated disaster, the economy went to hell, and people were confined to their homes and scared of each other. Safety guidelines within companies needed updating. At this point in her career, she wanted safety changes to be her legacy, not the disaster of MVoneshot.

"In conclusion, the FDA experts, across the board, reviewed in exquisite detail the application submitted by the Sponsor and found the safety and efficacy data consistent with a recommendation for approval of MVoneshot. It should also be noted that an outside panel of experts convened 6 weeks earlier reviewed the same package of data and voted unanimously, 13-0, to recommend approval to the Agency. I thank you for your attention."

Congressman Kenneth Carlin, Maryland, Chairperson:

"Thank you, Dr. Lansing. As chairperson of the House Committee on Crime, Terrorism and Homeland Security, I have one question for you or your colleagues before any other of the Members might want to begin with their questioning. How in the heck does a piece of the Bornavirus RNA get into a live measles virus vaccine and remain undetected and released into the market?"

As Dr. Lansing started to answer the question, she felt many emotions. Years in the FDA and nothing like this had happened under her watch. Everything was always done by the book. She really did not like the tone of the question, but nothing could be done about that now.

"Congressman, I am not in a position to answer that question, and neither is my staff. We approved the MVoneshot Vaccine, the unadulterated vaccine. This vaccine, according to all our tests did not contain this piece of RNA at the time of approval. We only discerned this small piece of RNA in samples obtained from lots of vaccine received after approval. I think it best to ask the Company this question," said Dr. Lansing.

"Very well, we will take this up with Immunoviratherapeutics after the break. Thank you. Let us recess for lunch."

1 PM

Chairperson Carlin

"I recall Dr. Ickerson for further testimony, and remember, sir, you are still under oath," said Carlin, "Dr. Ickerson, I will repeat the question that I presented to Dr. Lansing just before the break, how did a piece a totally different virus, the Bornavirus, find its way into MVoneshot?"

"Senator Carlin and respected committee members, this information came to light to us last week when the Agency, the FDA, informed us of their findings. We did not evaluate any RNA gene sequences in lots of the vaccine once released since this testing was not part of the quality control process. There would be no reason to look for Bornavirus or any other RNA virus for that matter,"

Ickerson answered, "In our investigation after the events, we have evaluated growth patterns of the corrupted measles vaccine in tissue culture and animal testing. The growth of the virus in the lab was consistent with all prior tests and release tests for the vaccine."

"The extra testing performed on animals was problematic. The lots of vaccine released caused central nervous system disease in some of the mouse and guinea pig model systems used. Based on these tests, we think a neurotropic measles strain, one that invades the brain, had been substituted with the proper vaccine. Original work in our labs ruled out using such a measles strain because it caused such adverse events in animals. Dr. Mazer and an insider, who we now know, performed this monstrous switch."

Senator Carlin interrupted, "The Committee knows that Dr. Mazer and an insider in your company to whom you refer replaced the benign vaccine strain with a killer neurotropic vaccine. No mix-up occurred. The Committee now wishes to understand how a piece of the Bornavirus gene wound up in your measles virus vaccine."

"I can only speculate. We only just found out last week when the FDA determined that a segment of the Bornavirus gene was contained in the MVoneshot vaccine. The FDA sequenced the entire vaccine gene and found extra RNA sequences compared to those in the original vaccine lots submitted to the Agency, as reviewed with you this morning. Using sophisticated supercomputers and artificial intelligence, they compared the extra RNA sequence to all other RNA sequences in multiple RNA databases. In that manner, the Agency found a small segment of the Bornavirus p24 RNA coding for the virus p4 protein sequestered within the MVoneshot vaccine RNA."

"We would never have looked for or tested for this in our release methods since it was not in our protocols and should not have been in the vaccine. We do not know how it was inserted, and I do mean inserted. Bornavirus infects many animals, both invertebrates and vertebrates, but the disease mainly affects horses and sheep. It is spread by the respiratory route and causes behavioral and neurologic abnormalities in many species. The virus, in rare instances, can infect humans and when it does, may cause psychiatric and neurologic disorders," Ickerson continued, "The piece of RNA attached to the measles genome did not have any effect on the replication of the measles vaccine, and did not impair the immune response to the vaccine. By itself, the small piece of RNA could not cause a Bornavirus infection. Based upon what we know from the literature; this is only a fragment of a protein of the Bornavirus. We need to read the sequence and determine if it has any function. As it is, it is just a small piece of the p24 protein."

"What will this tell the scientists?"

Ickerson responded, "This vaccine, as I said, has some bad properties. We know what happened when the vaccine was given to children and teens. Our animal work suggests that certain proteins might be the culprits. We do not know if it was a consequence of the measles virus or the extra piece of Bornavirus protein that had been inserted. We are checking our stocks of viruses and tracking down the original problematic strain that we thought was the only problem introduced by Mazer. If we have a Bornavirus protein to deal with, then that is another challenge. Such a protein, if active, might, according to some literature, lead to major issues in persons who received our tainted product. The protein might have caused many of the neurologic disorders seen acutely after the vaccine was administered."

Carlin added, "It seems to me we may need to get the Department of Justice involved here and have Dr. Mazer questioned yet again. After these hearings, I will follow up. Let's have additional questions for Colonel Ickerson from other members of the Committee."

14

Mean Man Hunt Explodes

March 2022

Alilah wondered if Kurt's investment in their travel to Saudi Arabia and the time, energy and money working on upgrading the Mean Man Hunt game would pay off. She hoped he would not be disappointed in this tactic and its ability to recruit more persons into NNA. Alilah honestly wished Kurt retained his good mood as they traveled the world. They began to have strong personal feelings for each other, and she wanted the relationship to grow into something more than a working connection. So far, she suspected he thought the same. And, she finally understood that her current husband, Alan Mazer, would be forever incarcerated; she knew they also had lost their love for each other years ago. Alilah had her twins back in the States and entrusted her parents to love and care for them.

Did this whole online crazy hate game thing keep the real edges of society engaged? Would these computer gamers deploying a pack of hate-filled mercenaries in the real world translate to any field successes? She hoped so, not only for their overarching plans but also for Kurt to see success with her as they worked together.

Meanwhile Alilah watched as the popularity of the game started to swell as it was made easier. Tens of thousands of individuals plotted nasty activities. Most of the real-life activities discussed never really happened, but the chats were lively and kept everyone amused with each other. The online game, multiple board discussions and videos on the internet gave a reality to the games and their plots. Even persons who started out playing just for potential monetary rewards may have refocused and changed their political views after participating in the "Game". Kurt's hope of accelerating hate online seemingly began to come to fruition.

Kurt and Alilah viewed the most daring of crimes through a very tightly controlled gaming portal. Alilah saw several daring individuals taking chances in real life. The one in particular from Paris impressed her. This young man attended sabbath services at a synagogue on a Friday evening and arranged a "shooting" to scare the entire Jewish population. During the beginning of the Sabbath service, everyone stands and turns to the door to greet the Sabbath Bride. This man arranged for his compatriot to shoot him from the entryway with a blank and for a blood pack to be released from his chest. He fell, rolled and as the congregation panicked, he escaped. Watching together, Kurt and Alilah began to select individuals, including this man. Kurt would have preferred, however, that he had not used a blank and had shot at congregants. These were the type of men and women who could supplement the current leadership force in the NNA.

Approximately one thousand verified videos had substantial payoffs. Of the hate crimes committed and not detected by authorities, about one hundred persons showed the ability to produce and lead attacks. These were the leaders Kurt and Alilah wished to recruit. It did not take long for his generals from the Americas, Europe, Africa, and Asia to reach out and connect with all of them. Before long, they became Lieutenants in the NNA. Of course, the other 900 people would not be overlooked. They too had useful qualities and might eventually be recruited as soldiers in the NNA.

The top one hundred individuals communicated through coded game channels only, were sent instructions on how, when and where to relocate. No communication with friends or family was allowed after joining the group; these individuals essentially dropped immediately from the face of the earth and moved upon the demand of the NNA. Each person went to a location remote from their current position so as not to be recognized. At these new places they underwent training in camps around the world by current NNA forces put in place over the last twenty years.

The travel to these locations would be slow and difficult, and some would not get there. For those that arrived, these new lieutenants of the NNA would help plan specific, new and more dramatic attacks against Jewish, homosexuals, Blacks, and the disabled. As he had hoped, Mean Man Hunt paid large dividends for Kurt's growing army. An organized group, not just groups of marauders running rampant, would now be on the ground under the direction of his generals. Alilah and Kurt now expected many victories in the field.

15

Investigations Continue

August 2021

Most of the U.S. Government and worldwide agencies gave up on finding Sabina Mazer. At this point, trying to determine her role in the 2018 virus attacks in the Jordan Olympics and the 2019 corrupted measles virus vaccine that killed and maimed thousands of children around the world was low on the priority list. But one investigator, Dr. Nari Lee, now with the CIA, did not yield. She had worked for the biotechnology company that developed the important breakthrough vaccine that could have helped millions of children around the world. Nari thought to herself that she could still be working in that biotechnology company or another, keeping her head to the ground and not paying much attention to world events. But that was not her style. Nari was all in. The world had increased in madness - killings, regional wars, and now even more possible biological attacks.

Nari was glad to be back in New England as a CIA operative. She had more than an inkling that Mazer had something else planned, even though his original biological attacks were performed years ago. A cold trail for most investigations, she hoped to heat this one up quickly.

Nari's highly secretive work took her to this area of the country to follow one specific area: Sabina's family. Sabina ran off and left her kids. She had not come back now for two years. Sabina had to be planning something, somewhere. Nari felt if it were her, she would have tried somehow to slip back to see her children. Could Sabina be elsewhere in the U.S. doing that planning. Or is she really a cold-hearted woman that left her young children never to return to the States, hiding out who knows where under a different name, with a new look?

The mosque had to be further investigated she thought. How could she have gotten out of the country without its help. Sabina had access to plenty of money, so buying a plane ticket would not have been a problem. Her husband had a solid position and income before screwing up and getting caught. He was a well-respected physician at a major medical institution and hospital in Baltimore. She worked. Money could not have been a problem. A team within or associated with the mosque or a terrorist group could have constructed a new identity and a passport readied for Sabina.

So, what was next. Sabina gone now for close to two years, must have hooked up with an international terrorist organization with the same militant Islamic views. The CIA field agent work to date had not turned up any sign of her in Somalia, Southeast Asia, Pakistan, Afghanistan, Egypt, Jordan or several other Arab states on the gulf. A wide area was searched, but she could have gone to any number of places that the Agency didn't have the resources to cover. Sabina was just one person and now only a suspect.

There were also nation-states that the U.S. agents would need the deepest of cover to enter or rely on informers to obtain reliable data. However, the Agency still considered Sabina a potential threat and felt she must be involved in some plan of attack or attacks on America or Israel. The Mossad had no hint as to where Sabina might be. Clearly, her husband's undertaking and science "experiments" with two nasty, deadly viruses looked like just the beginning. Nari's boss knew they needed to track her down and not delay any longer. Two years was certainly long enough.

Nari's initial work started with Sabina's trail to the mosque in Baltimore, where she worked for years. The Imam told the FBI and the JTTF that he had coincidentally loaned his car to Sabina on the day that Dr. Mazer tried to flee the country. The vehicle was spotted in photos on closed-circuit highway cameras along Route 1 from Baltimore all the way to Connecticut. After that, the track went cold.

Nari lived in Rhode Island for many years during her university days and knew that area of New England well. She liked to call this area of the country her second home. A California girl, she never moved back close to her workaholic parents in San Francisco. Her parents loved her, for sure, but never put out a strong message for her to move home. Instead, she stayed and became an Easterner, or more specifically, a New England woman at heart.

The trail really didn't go cold; rather, the FBI let it almost freeze over right away, taking little initiative. Sabina, from Revere, Massachusetts, a northern suburb of Boston, seemed likely to leave her children with her parents before disappearing. Nari determined this was true, and the Bureau did just a cursory interview of the parents and left. No follow-up was ascertained afterward. Further, they never checked the airport personnel. One could get to Logan, a major international airport, from Revere in less than thirty minutes in light traffic. Everyone knew this information, yet nothing was done to interview all the international flight agents or TSA personnel working that day. Sabina would never have used her own name.

Camera images of those boarding international flights could have easily been evaluated at the time or even shown to ticket agents working those flights. Nari thought it was time to review what had happened in 2019. She planned to interview all these agents at Logan International Airport who worked the day that Sabina left the country. Images were long gone and taped over. Prior interviews with her parents suggested she dropped her kids off and that Sabina left almost immediately that day. Nari intended to also speak with Sabina's parents. They had cooperated previously and certainly would cooperate again. They also wanted their daughter back. Of course, they did not know, nor did the JTTF know for certain, if Sabina had been involved in Dr. Mazer's virus attacks on the world.

On a mild December evening, the news broke of the mass shooting in Providence. Nari felt devastated. She spent years in Rhode Island going to Brown University and the University of Rhode Island. Now this event, on top of so many others, really hit home to her as she had often shopped in the same downtown Providence Place Mall.

That night, Nari awoke with an epiphany. Three years, three years, she thought. It had been almost three years since Mazer introduced the corrupted vaccine into the population. Could Mazer have planted something else in this vaccine that killed and maimed those children? She scratched out a note on the pad on her night table in large letters…. THREE YRS…WHAT ELSE?? She barely slept at all the rest of the evening; the killings in Providence and the thought that the vaccine might have something to do with the huge increase in violence really had her infuriated. She may have been the only person to put this together for the first time. She looked at the note on her bedside table, and so many other thoughts came to her mind as she awoke.

She started thinking back to her first classes in graduate school. The professor teaching the virology section to her introduction to microbiology course left a lasting impression on her.

She began to know him very well because of her immediate interest in the varied virus structures and how they might impact a host's immune response. She first went to meet with him just to discuss the geometry of certain viruses. However, discussions quickly became philosophical. Were viruses a life form? They could not live on their own. They needed to infect other hosts. They were bags of DNA or RNA ready to get into another animal and spread.

One particular chat that really stayed with Nari had to do with hatred and its relationship to viruses. Robinson told her one afternoon that his parents escaped the Holocaust. When they came to the United States, they legally changed their name from Rosenstein to Robinson. They had no idea what might be in store for them or their sons here but did not want to take any chances. The Robinsons did not wish to assimilate fully into American culture; they wanted to practice their Judaism, but they did not want to tempt fate. They felt safe in America and wanted to raise a family and keep them safe.

Dr. Robinson related to Nari the stories that his parents told him about the hate that began in Germany and Austria and grew over time in the 1930s. She knew only some history from childhood friends in grammar school but no details. Now, she learned from him the horrendous particulars, his family circumstances, other family stories, breakups, heartaches and deaths that so many Jewish families faced. Robinson related to her many of those specifics that his parents passed to him, an American-born citizen.

Dr. Robinson, after getting his doctorate in the 1960s during the civil rights movement and studying viral diseases, began to see similarities between hate and viral epidemics in man. They both start out very slowly. He told her they both take time to grow and then spread. Over time, the hate, or the virus, spreads from one person to another. Soon, many people become infected with the same material, passing it on to one generation and the next. Children develop that hate and do not even understand the reason. It can even remain latent and reignite.

She bolted upright in her bed. The Providence Place Mall. Nari had written down THREE YEARS in all upper-case letters in the middle of the night. So, another virus; Mazer must have placed another virus or piece of virus in the vaccine for a downstream disruption, she thought. It had nothing to do with the acute encephalitis symptoms seen in kids after injection of the vaccine. That had been the hypothesis put forward by the teams at the FDA and the Company in their testimony. This was a second attack going on in the brains of children and young adults. Now she had to prove this.

Nari was on her way to Massachusetts but needed to speak to Michael Hardy, her boss, to get some sense of what he wished her to do because she had her own ideas. She desperately wanted to be in on the interrogation of Mazer, but also wanted to be on the trail of Sabina. She wanted to be in both places.

In the morning, first thing, she called Michael. "Good morning, Michael. Nari here," she said.

"I know that voice. A little early. What can I do for you? I thought you were heading up to speak to the Imam in Baltimore this morning," he said.

"I want to speak with you about that. I think I should start in Boston. Get to the parents first, maybe even the kids if possible and then head to the airport. I know that's a long shot," Nari said.

"Why the change; why not start here first?" Michael asked.

"From what I've read, the people at the mosque, including the Imam, have been tight-lipped, and that includes two visits by the JTTF. No useful information on Sabina's whereabouts or her role in Mazer's plots came to light during those meetings," she said.

"So, you go to Boston, you question the family, who has been cooperative, and maybe you get some bit of information the FBI did not, and you go the airport and bring along a whole slew of lieutenants to help you. It has been a couple of years. Personnel have changed over often. No way we will get anything useful at Logan Airport," Michael said, "That is a waste of time."

"Please hold on a minute, I agree for the most part. But we have to assume she left on an international flight at a certain time. I will limit my questioning to staff who still work for airlines that were flying between 5 to 8 PM out of Logan that evening. I may get lucky. I will show her photo around and see if, by chance, any ground or flight personnel might remember her. It is a very long shot, I agree," Nari concluded.

"Actually, it is not as long a shot as you think. Her passport photo should be scanned into a database. Many of the airlines now use facial recognition when checking in for a flight. If she checked in on one of those airlines we could be in luck and will know her first destination. The name must match her face. I am surprised no one has done this, and we can do this right here," he said, "Get on a plane to Boston, go see the parents, and I will let you know how the photo matching goes. Have a good flight."

And with that, Nari called for an Uber at her townhouse in Vienna, Virginia and began her trip to Reagan National Airport. She pretty much knew the flight schedule by heart and could count on open seats at this time of day on several Boston flights. Parking at the airport was never easy, and depending upon the time of her return, she gave herself an option to which airport she would return. On her way, she called the Farooq's home, Sabina's parents, to introduce herself and requested time to speak with them either today or tomorrow. They were pleased to hear from her and excited after so long that someone was again following up on their "lost' daughter. Why had it taken so long, they almost cried on the phone together.

Michael had no luck with facial recognition. Not one hit. Not all airlines used facial recognition, but almost all flights leaving the U.S. did, so the result pained the team at Langley. Sabina used either tons of makeup, somehow changed her look, or possibly took a domestic flight to another city before leaving the country. In such a case, tracking down her whereabouts in the world just became a task of even magnitude greater.

Upon her arrival at the Farooq's home, the three of them exchanged pleasantries. They sat and talked in the living room for a while, speaking about Sabina.

"It has been so long, what could have happened to our Sabina?" asked Johara, almost breaking into tears.

"Mrs. Farooq, this case remains active. Do not give up hope. I came here to further investigate. Do you or Mr. Farooq remember anything about the woman she planned to meet? Do you recall if she said anything about her politics?"

"As I told the FBI before, Sabina stayed here very briefly. She barely said hello to us," said Fadi, "I don't know how else we can help."

"Did you know that Sabina worked at a mosque connected to radicalized Muslims, and we now believe may have been involved with financing terrorist activities against the United States?"

"No, no, no….my Sabina would not be involved in such evil work. We are all good Americans," Johara cried out.

"It is possible that Sabina has been involved in such activities for a long time, even from her high school days when she took a semester overseas," said Nari. Both of her parents sat and looked at each other bewildered.

"Do you think Sabina might have kept any notes or letters from her?" Nari said, even though she knew most correspondence these days came via email, it might still be possible that her friend Alice Germaine could have mailed her something."

"Maybe," Mr. Farooq answered.

"If you give me permission, I can conduct a search of your house without a warrant. However, it's crucial to ensure that your consent is given willingly and without any coercion. If you have concerns about a search, it's advisable that you consult a lawyer to understand your rights," Nari explained.

"No, I am fine with that. You go ahead. We have nothing to hide, and we have not touched Sabina's room since she left and married," he said, "We want to find Sabina."

Johara also agreed, nodding her head.

"Great. Thank you. I will look through her personal effects to attempt to find any items or clues that might help us. You can accompany me if you would like. I might want to take some things with me," she said.

"Okay. Let me first bring you to her room upstairs," said Fadi.

They headed to the second floor, and Nari began her search.

"It's a good thing it's a school day. The last thing I want is more disruption in the lives of Aamir and Najah," said Fadi upon returning to his wife.

As Nari entered the room, she noticed immediately that the whole area appeared untouched and looked like the bedroom of an older teenager. She searched Sabina's room for the better part of an hour, finding nothing. No paper, no old discs, no thumb drives, no papers, and, importantly, no letters from France were discovered. She searched between drawers, looked under cabinets, and found no hidden drawers or sequestered spaces. A completely clean area, and nothing remotely related to a person who had ever been to France or any European destination could be found in that room. Nari now wondered about Sabina's story from her high school days and onward. She told her parents she had spent half a year in Paris with this friend, whatever her name was, and now no evidence existed she had even been there. Her school records showed she had not been to France, and her expired passport was not there, but it would be easy to check the European records for entry into any European country since these data were kept electronically. It might be useless but it would be a restart on this investigation, she thought.

Nari thanked the Farooq's for their time and told them she would check the Euro data base for Sabina's arrival as a teen. As Nari began to leave, Mrs. Farooq teared up. Nari turned back. She gave her some last bit of hope.

"We still have to interview airport personnel and look at images on the day she left. That information could give us leads on where Sabina went on the first leg of her trip," Nari, showing some compassion, said, "It's a long shot, but we are not giving up yet."

Nari then took off for the Holiday Inn by the airport, her next destination. She knew the facial recognition was another gamble but something that they needed to check. After a loud overnight stay with aircraft flying overhead all night at the hotel, Nari returned to DC the next morning and took a more comfortable role as a scientist/agent at the CIA headquarters.

Now Nari was back in her zone. She began to reanalyze data related to the previous vaccine virus attack on the United States. She had concerns that something beyond the acute effects of the vaccine that maimed and killed children and teens might have been entangled within the measles vaccine, now known as the corrupted MVoneshot. Dr. Mazer, now in for life in Federal Prison, had mutated the virus. It killed children and caused severe neurologic disease in many others. Adults and teens who took it did not have any severe symptoms; many took it just to be safe and to boost their immunity to the measles virus. Her thoughts turned to Mazer's background in neurovirology and the esteemed lab in which he had trained.

Nari knew that some viruses could cause persistent or silent infection and then go on to cause active disease years after infection. Some viruses might not even cause signs of acute infection, and then many years later could show up as a problem. The herpes simplex viruses everyone knew about. Once infected, always infected. It would pop out on the lips or genitals at the most inconvenient times. Same with the virus that causes chickenpox, varicella zoster, which is a virus of childhood. That virus could recur in adulthood as herpes zoster and be especially painful, especially in older persons. And HIV, which eventually can cause AIDS, persists for life once infected.

Nari had followed the work from Mazer's lab. She had to know what he did; he was criminally insane. In her previous role as a Medical Scientist with Immunoviratherapeutics, she provided him with information about upcoming developments, if he would give her the time of day. She knew all the important concepts related to the immune responses to vaccines and the nervous system, especially viruses on which Mazer worked. She thought his training made it easier to develop deleterious vaccines. He could have tweaked a vaccine that could protect kids into one that harms them. It would not have been very difficult for Mazer or his co-conspirator to have inserted or modified a piece of viral RNA into the vaccine. He knew from his study of the measles virus and work in neurology that a very severe form of measles infection called SSPE, subacute sclerosing panencephalitis happened sometimes.

It affected the brain when a mutation in one portion of the measles virus M protein occurred. When this happened, the virus persisted in the brain for a while and persons developed SSPE, a uniformly fatal disease. This disease starts out about 3 to 9 years after natural measles infection. It usually begins with mild memory loss, change in behavior and then loss of motor function, such as uncontrollable muscle movements (jerking motions). Some people would not be able to walk as their muscles will become spastic. After deterioration to a vegetative state, patients die as the brain will not be able to control bodily function.

On one hand, developing a modification of a measles protein code and inserting it into the RNA of the vaccine sounded like something Mazer might have attempted with Ashraf, his man in the Company, who had the skills. But Mazer concerned himself about the acute effects of the vaccine and needed to look into other ways to change the vaccine, beyond its direct neurovirulence. He had already known the virus they selected to replace the approved vaccine would have a direct kill effect on many children. He needed something with a delayed effect, she thought.

All the time she worked, Nari had one ear tuned to the Congressional hearings. She knew all the details. Ickerson, the CEO of Immunoviratherapeutics and Lansing, the FDA Director, went on with their long and drawn-out reviews of the details and background of the MVoneshot vaccine. This hearing was no place for subordinates to present information.

Nari turned her attention to other RNA viruses that Mazer might try to integrate into the measles RNA gene that could cause a delayed affect. Nari began to evaluate the CDC's reports of unusual events and a national registry of adverse events for the last several years since the new MVoneshot vaccine had been introduced and then quickly taken off the market. Could Mazer have introduced a chronic illness into society? It was a time bomb ready to explode.

If any disorders or diseases increased in specific groups or in specific areas, Nari figured she could trace these back to vaccine distribution and injection if that's what caused the events. With the advent of fast computers and Artificial Intelligence, she could ask any number of questions and get her answers almost immediately. She knew some of the data was not reliable. The adverse event information reported to the FDA was only as good as the reporter, and in many cases, the patients were reporting information that was vague and not helpful. She started to put in query after query and evaluate result after result. Nari thought she started to see patterns but then thought, "maybe I am crazy."

She remembered an old Showtime series from 15 years earlier, Homeland, where the star, Claire Danes, a CIA agent, saw all these patterns in her work, and she was a manic-depressive, off her rocker. But in the end, she could be right. Nari kept on working right through lunch and into the evening, seeing more and more patterns.

A little after the lunch break the next day in the Congressional Hearings, despite her exhaustion, Nari's ears perked up. She heard the word "Bornavirus" and immediately stopped her work. She backed up the streaming testimony and listened again to what Ickerson had said. He did say "Bornavirus". The FDA had found a piece of Bornavirus RNA in the MVoneshot vaccine. The FDA had screened all the RNA databases available and detected a piece of the RNA that would make part of the p24 Bornavirus protein within the measles vaccine.

Nari thought, "This is exactly what I have been looking for; it was not SSPE. It was not a neuropathogenic measles that Mazer planted but a totally different virus for the second attack. What a coy bastard, sitting right there in prison waiting and watching this happen!"

First things first, she thought. It was time to bone up on everything Bornavirus and p24. What does this p24 protein do within the virus life cycle, and by itself, can it have any effect on host cells? Her first call tomorrow would be to Ickerson, her old friend and former CEO at Immunoviratherapeutics, just down the road from Langley in Vienna, VA. Who would not accept a visit from the CIA? And, then, on to the High-Security Federal Prison in Lee County where Dr. Mazer spends his days now. Can the Government charge him with more crimes if other problems are found in the same vaccine that he already adulterated? Who takes the lead on this investigation?

Nari started by reviewing recent publications on Bornavirus infections in humans. She used the PubMed database, which contained almost all medical and biological works published around the globe and available through the National Library of Medicine. She also checked open-access articles, those that had not yet been peer-reviewed but were still available for reading. She was surprised at the volume of work done on this little talked-about virus, a virus that infected so many species of animals. It rarely infected humans but certainly could. Journal articles published on human Bornavirus disease did catch Nari's attention. Titles like "Schizoaffective disorders in patients and their families" and "Neuropathogenesis of persistent infection with Bornavirus disease virus" jumped out at her. Clearly, Dr. Mazer had thought this through thoroughly and knew quite a lot about Bornavirus disease in humans even though he "attacked" the population with a deadly acute measles virus vaccine.

Nari, on the right track, continued to look at adverse events in the United States collected by the FDA. She delved into anything related to the brain and the MVoneshot vaccine usage. Companies must report to the FDA serious and unexpected adverse events immediately and other serious events on a periodic basis. These were quite solid data and picked up important trends. The Vaccine Adverse Event Reporting System (VAERS) database, a U.S.-wide system, could capture any reported events. VAERS accepted information reported by doctors, nurses as well as laypeople, with as much or as little data inputted into the system as provided. A great idea, but flawed in that anyone could submit these events.

Nari took a break and looked at the news on her laptop. More of the same, she thought. Israeli and Palestinians were at it over

West Bank territories, and China was continuing to threaten Taiwan, North Korea exploded more missiles off the east coast of South Korea, more suicides in young teens, the climate is heating up Atlantic, and expect more hurricanes than usual…She backed up and thought about the previous headline. "More suicides". Nari had seen this before, and had not paid any attention to it. Now this article, she re-examined, focused on younger kids, not older, depressed adults.

Something clicked, and she began to think whether this suicide headline might be a long-term or chronic consequence of the MVoneshot vaccine in older children. The limbic regions of the central nervous system, contained those nerve cells in the brain largely responsible for emotions and mood disorders. She had just read almost everything available on Bornavirus and the nervous system. If this virus did attack the brain, it could cause acute encephalitis or possibly a long, drawn-out disease. A quick literature review gave her some information.

Nari found one set unusual of papers published in obscure journals. All were published in Eastern European journals, with only English abstracts, so she could not get too much detail. But the bottom line was key. When chimpanzees were injected with the Bornavirus p24 protein, things turned ugly; the animals became angry, started fight responses, and had vocalization responses. Could this protein be causing havoc in young children's brains? It could be changing all sorts of neuroendocrine effects inducing stress hormones as well. Might this be the cause of the increased violence and craziness seen everywhere in the country and around the Western world? Or was this just a coincidence?

All she knew now was that lots more work was needed. Nari hyped up only on her discoveries, moved to the kitchen and brewed a fresh pot of coffee. She felt at this time she had to carry on. Sleep had to wait so she could continue to dive deeper into this mystery. As the hours ticked away, the studies she read confused her, but she could not tell if it was from lack of sleep, poorly designed studies, or just inconsistent effects of Bornavirus.

In her sleep-deprived state, Nari came up with a plan to evaluate whether these psychiatric manifestations in vaccinated persons were due to Bornavirus. She needed to contact the best neuropathologists. These docs would need to evaluate brain tissue from those persons who shot or exploded bombs or otherwise died in the act of committing crimes against the population. Nari knew where to take these tissues next. She had a close colleague who had the technical ability to look for pieces of Bornavirus RNA or protein in brain tissue. One call and Nari could arrange for the samples to be sent to a lab at the University of California, Davis, Institute for Evaluation of Neurodegenerative Diseases. This lab had the wherewithal to identify almost any occult virus protein or RNA in the brain.

The next day Nari got shot down by her boss's boss. Martin Erlich called Nari Lee to his office first thing the next morning. "Nari, I have read your mind, and the answer is NO. I know you have lots of academic contacts from your previous life, but you must listen to me and Michael on this. First, there is a chain of command, and your boss is here in the room. Normally, you would go directly to your station chief in the field or, in this case the director of your division, Michael," Erlich said, "We have known each other many years now, and I convinced you to join the Agency. Second, we will not have anyone outside the government handling or testing these brain samples. I'm telling you to go to your director on where to have those samples tested. Let's just say UCSD is not in play."

I guess he did not read my mind, she concluded, the head of the CIA watches over all. I cannot do a thing on my computer without my good friend checking in. Nari felt devastated but should have known better.

"Wow. Yes, sir. I planned on only going to the best…"

Nari was cut off. "Just stop right there. We have protocols in place for good reason and speak to Michael right after this meeting. He is here to guide you. He can give you all the details, and there will be no more shortcuts."

"Got it, and I'm on my way. Thank you for the advice," and Nari left the office immediately.

In a matter of minutes, Nari stood at Hardy's door. As she walked into his office, she started to explain why the UCSD lab was the premier lab for the detection of brain viruses. Erlich had already read him in on the whole situation and of course, had known the directive. He stopped her immediately after she began her rationale for sending the samples out. He was not enraged but upset that she did an end run around him during this whole investigation. And now she wished to speak to him about the lab that the boss had clearly cut out.

"Nari, I have been at this job a long time and I plan to keep it. The Agency has resources that many of us do not know exist. First and foremost, this investigation will not leave the government auspices and head into an academic setting. Right now, it stays within the government. Obviously, when the Bornavirus contamination in the vaccine came to the forefront at the FDA testimony during the open Congressional hearings, the public became on edge. Every scientist, pseudoscientist and correspondent develop theories as to what could happen. Now this can't occur as it did after the initial measles debacle. We are investigating what most of the world has forgotten. News cycles help us. The last thing we need is more outside groups involved and potentially leaking information," Michael explained.

"I understand. So how and when can we arrange to get the brain tissue sent to us or to wherever you suggest. It will need to be tested in certain sections, which we will specify, for both p24 protein and p24 RNA," Nari asked, "And, these tissues that we receive from various autopsy brain samples might be formalin-fixed."

"I am not sure what that means... you will have to discuss with the lab where I will be sending you and the samples," said Michael.

"There might be other issues as well. Also, a scientific issue, our investigation seeks to find just pieces of the protein or RNA, since we think Dr. Mazer probably only inserted just a segment of the Bornavirus code into the measles virus," Nari summarized.

"Well, again, talk to the science people. You will head up I270 to Frederick, MD, to Fort Detrick. Your former boss, Colonel Ickerson, actually has great connections there as well. The lab, home of our country's biological defense organization, otherwise known as USAMRIID, United States Army Medical Research Institute of Infectious Diseases, will certainly work and collaborate willingly with you," said Michael, "We arranged this collaboration for other potential infectious attacks on America."

"Thanks, Michael, and yes, Dr. Ickerson worked for several years at Frederick while in the Air Force. I visited the lab in the past and I know several scientists there. I have not met anybody who worked on Bornavirus," Nari responded, "Do you have the direct contacts for me?'

Michael said, "You can discuss all the details with Dr. Allison Bailey. She will await your call. I will save you a little time, so you don't have to do any research on her. She went to undergrad at Harvard, received her medical degree and doctorate at Stanford in molecular biology, and did a three-year postdoctoral fellowship at the University of California, Davis, Department of Neurology. Allison then joined the Army as a lieutenant colonel to work with USAMIIRD. She is currently assigned to the Fort Detrick team, studying persistent virus infections causing neurologic disease. Her contact information is in this file."

"Thank you, Michael; I will not disappoint," Nari said, and with that, she left his office and returned two levels down to her own desk.

"Allison won't either," he said in a loud voice as she left.

16

More Bornavirus Investigations

August 2021

Michael headed back to Erlich's office. "I do not anticipate any further problems with Nari," Hardy said, "She will handle the tissue procurement and analysis as per our orders. The tissue goes to Fort Detrick, as we wanted all along."

"Thanks, Michael. Now these prepubescent and older teens seem to me to be only one part of the problem," Erlich continues, "Many of the shootings we've seen were carried out by adults. I think we have another issue to deal with. Who organized these seemingly unrelated shootings and gang violence?"

"What are your thoughts now?" asked Michael.

"Unfortunately, my thoughts probably don't mean much. In any case, unrelated to this Bornavirus crap, I think anyone could be perpetrating these actions," said Erlich, "Yes, anyone, including internal hate groups, and there are many sleeper cells, individual nut jobs, the list is long. And there's a lot more I am worried about. The FBI will have to investigate, but you probably heard the entire Congressional hearings. What else can happen to our drug and biological pipeline? Right under our noses a vaccine was corrupted.

This might have been a test case. I can only imagine what might happen next if this country can't get its act together. I have called for a meeting with the director of the FBI, Jonas Hamilton, myself, the head of the Drug Research and Development Organization and President Moreno to discuss this particular issue. If all pharma and biotech companies don't have this under control immediately, at all manufacturing sites worldwide, then our citizens will be open to attack, and our entire economy will be at risk."

"Sure enough boss and this meeting and action might be more important than our current work plan," Michael said.

"No, but just as important. You handle the current work. I am responsible for the big-picture stuff here. Now let's continue," Erlich said.

"Who has been studying and investigating ties to all the other shootings, explosions, and these random attacks, if that is what they are?" said Michael.

"That would be the Joint Terrorist Task Force and the FBI. This investigation does not fall under our domain. I need to check with the JTTF to see what they might have. They could give us some leads internationally also. Keep me updated on the virus thing and anything else you hear in the halls in our own Company and FDA," said Erlich.

"But to tell you the truth, there are lots of moving parts here. I think we are up against a Hydra. Do you know remember your Greek mythology, Michael?'

"A little," he said, "I think that's the monster with multiple heads that Hercules killed?"

"Yes, and right now, I think we are up against a Hydra, and we have not done a good job killing it. It grows more heads every time we try to eliminate one. With lots of heads and two more sticking its face right up into ours every time we get a lead on one of the other *heads*," said Erlich.

"Do we have enough resources?" asked Michael.

"They are spread thin. And now I have another thought. I still need to discuss additional work that Nari might have to do if you agree. Remember Ashraf, Ashraf Khaleed, the laboratory head in the vaccine company who Dr. Mazer killed?" he asked.

"Yes, but of course, we did not pay any attention to him. He was a patsy. Mazer killed him just before trying to escape the country. All along, you and the rest of the JTTF thought Ashraf handled Mazer's dirty work. He was just a lackey and carried out Mazer's work for him at Immunoviratherapeutics, switching the good vaccine for the bad," said Michael.

"But," said Erlich. "In retrospect he might be the lynchpin to the Bornavirus problem happening now. He had the background and training and performed much of the molecular biology to develop the original vaccine. He developed the MVoneshot before moving into manufacturing," said Erlich, "He, not Mazer, might have been the person responsible for thinking up a plan for adding another pathogen to the MVoneshot vaccine, after hooking up with Mazer."

"So, does it matter now who did it, the dead assistant or the guy in prison for what, thirty life terms?" said Michael.

"Oh, it matters. Do we know if Mazer planned it or Ashraf came up with it on his own makes a big difference? Mazer just directing Ashraf indicates no other persons had the intellect to do something like this in that Company. If Ashraf did this on his own, he might have had collaborators within the Company, now somewhere out and free, that we have not investigated. People we have not yet looked into. That comes later, after a thorough Mazer investigation. We may not be done with Immunoviratherapeutics," said Erlich.

"Right now, we need the FBI to issue a warrant for Mazer's arrest. Yes, he is in a Federal Penitentiary, but it is just procedural for the additional crime discovered. His counsel should be notified, and of course, before any questioning, Mazer needs to be read his Miranda rights as this is custodial interrogation."

"I did not think my day was going to start like this, but it's always like this here, that's why I love it and stay right here," Michael joked.

"Thanks, and have a good rest of the day, Michael," said Erlich.

"Well, I will try, but I do not have a good feeling about this. Kids killing themselves and shooting up a few schools is bad enough; now you're saying we could have a whole armed force out there. And we do not know who is controlling them. And the medicine I took for my blood pressure might kill me. Sure, I will try my best to have a good day," see you later, boss.

Later that day Michael received an encrypted message upon returning to his office. Two of his agents in Afghanistan had leads suggesting a connection to Sabina and were on their way from Kabul to the west of the country in Herat, bordering Iran. A long and dangerous journey for these two men traveling as Afghans. It may or may not end up with useful information or a connection to Sabina. On the surface, relations between Iran and Afghanistan, ever since the Taliban took control of Afghanistan, looked from the outside to be normalized. But a two-century old dispute between the countries still existed over water rights to the Helmand River at the border.

That dispute paled in comparison to their theological differences. Iran was largely Shiite, and Afghanistan was mostly a

Sunni Muslim country. The United States had no official diplomatic relations with Iran, still spinning centrifuges and developing nuclear materials in breach of the United Nations Nuclear Non-Proliferation Treaty. The same held true in Afghanistan since the Taliban took control, but the United States did have many deep cover assets in Afghanistan. It did seem ridiculous that the U.S. had no official relations, given that the country left behind billions of dollars' worth of military equipment and allies without any protection from the Taliban. Now, the CIA felt it was time to use its assets both within Afghanistan and Iran as well. All evidence pointed to Iran as one likely location of persons or groups running operations that continued to disrupt people in the United States and Western Europe.

17

Out On The Town

May 2021

Stuck living in the Virginia suburbs of DC gave Nari few prospects for meeting eligible men. In her mid-thirties and working either in the field or the confines of the office at Langley, where work required restricted speech, her chances of finding a date at the office were tough enough, forget getting into a long-term relationship. A Saturday night and, tired from the stress and hard work week she hemmed and hawed but finally called back her best friend. Nari and Amie, her roommate for the first two years of undergrad school at Brown University years ago, had hung out from time to time.

They went in opposite directions most of the time now, Amie to her scheduled lecturers at Georgetown Med and Nari with her unusual and unscheduled CIA duties, about which Amie knew nothing. If Amie wasn't lecturing or doing research in her genetics lab she had clinical attending responsibilities on the pediatric floors in the new Georgetown Pediatric Hospital.

Off to DC and the night spots on lower Wisconsin Ave, Nari and Amie went for the first time in many months, unsure where they would go or what they would really do. They were both very attractive women but certainly not the type expected to be hit on in a bar since they were not the youngest clients in the establishment. Without their current high-stress jobs they both would have probably been working and raising a family by now.

Finally, after getting through clogged M street traffic they made their way a few blocks north on Wisconsin and parked on the first side street they saw with an open spot. A bustling Saturday night left few spaces available. Nari and Amie walked just one block south and found a seat just outside the bar/restaurant at Warvins. Nari liked the available space since the seats faced the street and were pushed up against the wall of the building. A waiter came over almost immediately and asked for their drink order. Tonight qualified as the end of a tough week. Hard liquor was on the menu.

"Tito's on the rock's with a twist," Nari said.

Amie said, "Same for me."

Nari sat quietly for a few minutes, just relaxing after a long week, and then the drinks arrived."

"Thank you, bring two more," said Nari.

"I guess it will be a heavy drinking night. Was it a bad week? By the way, Nari," said Amie, "We haven't spoken in detail much since you left your job in in the biotech industry. I would like to know what you are doing."

"Amie, I think I've told you I am doing pretty much the same thing I did previously but as a consultant in the biopharma space," Nari said.

"Must pay pretty well. You're driving a new BMW, got yourself a nice townhouse in Vienna, and you don't skimp on the fashion," said Amie.

"I didn't think you paid attention to that stuff," said Nari.

"I do wear a lab coat, but hey, I still do wear other clothes underneath," said Amie.

"To get back to your question, though, it really has not been a great couple of years," she replied.

"Do you want to talk about it," asked Amie.

"I really can't," Nari said.

"We've known each other for what, fifteen years or more. If you can't talk to me…. oh forget it. Let's just toast to great days ahead."

The two of them clinked their glasses and took big drinks. Nari kept the glass in her hand and almost finished the whole drink before putting it back on the table.

"Here is some bread for the table," the waiter said, "I assume you will be dining with us."

"Yes, we will, but we will be drinking for a while first, taking it slow," said Amie. "Thanks."

Just then, Nari noticed two twenty-something guys waiting to get into the restaurant, gawking at them from the hostess stand. Nari, not in a great mood to begin with, stared right back at one.

She whispered to Amie, "Horses asses."

"Please don't get into with them; they are only kids, probably grad students at GW or Georgetown," said Amie.

"I'll try, but…

The 'kid' still stared at them while they drank.

"Hey bud, you can stop looking at me. I'm not your Tinder date; why don't you wait for your table over there. You are bothering us." Nari said loudly.

"Here are your other drinks," the waiter appeared at a good time.

"Thank you," they said in unison.

Amie had yet to finish her first drink, and Nari picked up her second Tito's and the 'kid' came closer, almost at her side, watching her drink.

"Didn't I say to get the fuck out of here," Nari shouted at him.

The sound of a sudden explosion made Nari and Amie jump from their seats as it shook the ground where they sat. Nari immediately took a few steps toward the street and saw a ball of flame to the south. By now most people also had stood up and moved to the edge of Wisconsin Avenue to see what had happened.

Nari looked back and did not see Amie at their table and assumed she was on the street with others. Nari then took off south down Wisconsin. She could tell from the smoke and fire trucks already headed in that direction that the explosion had come from the M-Street area, only several blocks from where they had started their evening.

Just across M sat a huge mall and condominium complex. The Shoppes at Georgetown Park was a possible target, she thought. Nari ran as fast as possible without tripping on cobblestones or old trolley tracks in her heels and drew her sidearm upon reaching the mall. She showed her CIA ID to the local cop on the scene, who had already called for backup. They heard sirens; response teams were on the way.

To Nari it appeared as if some explosive device had been detonated in the center of the building. Fire and smoke now spread in all directions, but mostly northerly, in the direction from where she had just run. There was no getting into that building now. People were still exiting from garage points and all doorways she could see. Nari stepped aside and called Amie.

"Amie, there has been an explosion at the mall," Nari said.

"I figured something like that; why did you take off like that?" Amie asked, "Are you alright?"

"Yes. I will be back in a little bit; I assume Lenny and Squiggy are gone?"

"Yes, with the wind," said Amie.

"See you soon."

Nari turned to the police officer, "There is nothing I can do here; your crew and the FBI will take over once the Fire Department slows down the burn to figure out what happened. Have a better rest of your shift."

"Thanks lady,"

At first, before heading back, Nari thought about staying at the site until investigators arrived. But she never witnessed anything other than smoke, as did the officer, and never came close to the building. With those thoughts in mind, she walked back up Wisconsin Avenue to the restaurant, wondering what she would tell Amie.

"Hi Amie, I am back,"

"I see. Now, why did you, of all people, a pharmacist and immunologist, have to run to a blast in the middle of Georgetown?" Amie asked.

"Can I have another drink first?"

"Yes, drink your water first. Now tell me what's going on, 'consultant' who flies all over the world?" Amie asked again.

"Well, now I know. You must work for the CIA, correct?" Amie said.

"No, I do not work for the CIA or the FBI or any such people. And if I did, I could not tell you anyway. You would be at risk, my dear friend. I carry a gun because my current contract takes me into some bad areas. My contractor requires it of me." Nari explained.

"Okay, so why did you run down to M-Street?" asked Amie, "And why didn't I hear from you for the last ten months?"

"First, I thought I could help in some way. We do have training. I did not see you at the table and thought you may have gone there to provide medical assistance," said Nari, "and second, I apologize. I had a long, tense time in San Francisco for the last nine months. I had a long-term client there, and I tried to resolve my relationship with my parents. It took time, but now I know I just can't go back to them. I know it was self-centered. I should have told you. Can you forgive me?"

"Yes. But please don't pull this crap again, Nari," Amie said.

"And by the way, I was ready to kick the shit out of Lenny and Squiggy," Nari said, "I am hungry, now let's order."

"Nari, did you survive the night and wake sans headache," said Amie calling from her kitchen while making herself breakfast. Nari was usually an early riser, but she had the whole weekend off and stayed in bed until eight this morning.

"I did just fine. But I am not sure why you called me at, geez, it's 8:15 on a Saturday morning." Nari said, "Are you planning some great escape to Tysons Corner, it is a bit early?"

"No, but you promised me one day you would take me golfing. You, the high school and collegiate phenom, had a lot of promise, so time to pass that talent on to a friend," Amie said.

"First, it's too early in the morning to talk about this. Second, my talent is long gone, so you really need to see a professional instructor. And, I guess third, I have not touched a club for years. My clubs are rusting in the garage and lastly, why? You don't have time for this game. I'd rather have my coffee, and then we can talk about going out shopping."

"Well, what about teaching me how to shoot? Now that you carry a pistol, maybe I should get one, too? Crime is only rising everywhere," said Amie.

"Amie, stop it. I am not an instructor. I can barely hit the broadside of a barn. If you want a license for a handgun you need to go through the Virginia state requirements. Go to a range, get a real instructor to show you safety and how to use a gun properly," said Nari.

"Well just maybe today we can head over to Tysons Corner and target some of the stores there. You can't miss those, pun intended," said Amie.

"That's a date, but those stores open at eleven, and I am going back to bed. I will meet you then. It is too early now. Bye," said Nari.

18

The President Addresses Congress
March 2022

"In closing, I have never been a woman of many words. As I complete my State of the Union Address to Congress this evening, let me be clear, this message goes out to the world. We are not at war. We are at peace and will always be a nation of peace, but do not cross us. When people infiltrate our country with ideas of hate and poison our people, as they have recently, they too will be considered enemy combatants. Do not cross the line and break the laws of our country.

If you do, we must stop the madness. No group can attack us from within. We will not be forced or scared out of our nation by unknown "haters" of our people. Those who came here from far and wide made America. We came from varied backgrounds and from all continents. We are white, Black, red and yellow. We are Christian, Muslim, Jew, Hindu, and anything else we care to be. When you see thugs like those men wearing Nazi arm bands, what can you do in our country.

Educate them if they will listen to you. If they won't open their closed minds, smile and point to the majority. They are with you. The world is with you and not them, not the haters. We are the people of the nation and the world who work together and want to live in peace. Hate will not survive here. The haters and their leaders, whoever they are, hidden in bunkers, are not the persons desired and wanted in this country and world. Their kind only wishes to eliminate the truly good people of the world. With education going forward, we will stop the horrendous harassment that many of us have endured. With proactive education, we will prevent more problems. Go out and educate against hate. Education is the vaccine that will prevent and also treat this horrible disease of bigotry and hate. Anyone not receiving our vaccine against hate will not last long as a free person in America. It is not lawful to violate our rights and harm those of us who choose to be good citizens.

Good night, and may God bless the United States of America and its People. Thank you."

With that conclusion, Congresspersons from both sides of the aisle rose in unison, applauded and cheered the President's closing remarks.

19

Getting Up To Speed
December 2021

"**M**adame President, thank you for taking time from your busy schedule to meet with us today. We have a very important subject on which to brief you," said Martin Erlich

"Why was this not part of my daily briefing this morning?" asked the President

"This is too sensitive and impacts everything from financial markets to war plans to plans related to anti-terrorism planning. Your chief of staff is not in this room as she cannot hear all we have to say. I also have one other person I plan to bring into the meeting in a few minutes," said Erlich, "may I proceed."

"Yes, proceed," said President Julia Moreno as she took a sip of coffee.

"First, every pharmaceutical product we make here and around the world might be at risk to terrorist influence. Second, the original terrorist, Dr. Mazer, who corrupted the measles vaccine and deployed a dangerous virus at the Jordan Olympics, somehow also implanted a second virus in the measles vaccine," said Erlich.

"First, this should be in my daily briefing, and second, yes, the FDA Commissioner, in a private memo, advised me that there could be a problem with this Bornavirus thing. However, my understanding was that it could be months before anything could be confirmed along those lines. But even so, what would be the consequences of this piece of Bornavirus RNA?" asked the President.

"Our investigations have now found that it may have been activated in the brains of teens that did not die. Many commit suicide, and others seem to commit violent or aggressive acts. We have Agent Nari Lee to thank....."

"Not now, no praise now, please," the President interjected.

"And a rash of killings by young children in schools and elsewhere, as well as car crashes into crowds and other notable incidents can be related to activated virus segments in certain areas of the brain. The area where the virus pieces seem to go is the limbic system, the area responsible for emotion, memory, control of the endocrine system and other important function," Erlich concluded.

"So, what do we do now? Thousands of children and teens around the globe, but mostly here received this screwed-up vaccine. What's the action plan?" she said.

FBI Director Jonas Hamilton chimed in, "Madame President, nothing can be done at this time to eliminate the virus gene. We do have several companies working on treatments and testing them in model systems right now. One type of treatment is a monoclonal antibody against the p24 protein; the other is an inhibitor against the RNA, an inhibitory RNA called iRNA. As soon as we know that either can cross into the brain, we will be ready to test in normal volunteers. Other gene silencer treatments may come along as well. In summary, I think we are a year away from an experimental treatment."

"I understand why you wanted a limited meeting. Seems to me we have lots of issues to be worked out here, and honestly, worldwide problems that must be shared. My biggest concern is your treatment timeline. Who is in the wings?" she asked.

"We have brought in the President of the Drug Research and Development Group.

"Does he have a better timeline?" she interrupted.

"No. He, Dr. Sam Jones, will be able to speak for the manufacturers of pharmaceuticals in the U.S and their willingness to work with us. We have other issues affecting all of our pharmaceuticals. He is not privy to our current knowledge of Bornavirus and its relationship to the killings. However, this information must come out eventually. He understands our concern about probable terrorism in all manufacturing plants around the globe," said Erlich.

"Okay. Bring him in," she said.

"Madame President, may I introduce Dr. Samuel Jones, President of the Drug Research and Development Group," said Erlich.

"Dr. Jones, a pleasure to meet you. I know what a difficult job you have working with so many diverse companies. Welcome in this difficult time. I know both Mr. Hamilton and Mr. Erlich have briefed you on our meeting," the president stated.

"Yes, and thank you. We know the problems that could possibly occur, especially after the MVoneshot disaster. I have already assembled the leading manufacturers of pharmaceuticals and met with them to discuss the potential issues surrounding the manufacturing of products. We all agree this problem is beyond hypothetical," said Jones.

"So, after your first meeting, do you have any action items?" asked President Moreno.

"Yes, several. And we need to expand our work overseas. First, as you probably know, when manufacturing a drug product, several component products get delivered from multiple sources to a manufacturing facility and then to a final filling facility. Companies do not make each component of a drug, rather, they put them together and synthesize or blend the final drug product.

At these several steps along, potential problems could occur," Dr. Jones continued, "But all companies must test or obtain tests every step of the way. They must always ensure that components put into a product are absolutely pure such that the final pharmaceutical delivered is pristine. We believe strongly now the issue at hand relates to personnel. We might not have control of our personnel and personnel's behavior in contract facilities. We do not hire these individuals. The contractor hires based on credentials. If someone is intent on doing harm, then they will do harm. If someone has a certain belief or has been influenced by external sources or by a payment, we do not know how to control this behavior."

"I am asking for your action points, not the problems, Dr. Jones," said the President, "We are not about to change hiring practices overseas or here in the U.S."

"I apologize, but I needed to get the issue on the table," he said, "In the case of the measles vaccine fiasco, a company insider was persuaded by a sophisticated outsider, a radicalized Muslim activist, to switch the good for the bad vaccine. It took lots of expertise, but nonetheless…"

"So, with many holes in the system," President Moreno interrupted again in a louder voice, "I will ask once again…what steps are ongoing now to prevent our drug and biologic supply from another attack?"

"The group has a list of problems and each Company must report back as to how they intend to address these issues within thirty days. New employee hiring practices will be tighter and stricter guidelines and secure background testing will be undertaken on all hires." Jones said, "For current employees, action items include, for example, biweekly screening of employee patterns such as daily interactions with internal and external persons during the workday, emails on the company computers, web use, etc. Of course, home use cannot be monitored. The testing of each chemical ingredients and components used to manufacture each batch of drug product will be checked and double checked for contamination."

They all knew one overarching problem related to companies and contractors around the globe, notably in China and India. Europe might not be a problem, especially for manufacturers in Ireland, Italy and Belgium, but elsewhere in the EU could be. However, the big players in pharmaceutical contract manufacturing sat in China and India, and controls were not tight.

"Let's assume that everything gets monitored, right down to filling each pill or liquid vial, and now it is shipped to a warehouse. Who controls the storage and who monitors the pills at this point?' asked the President.

"This all depends upon the particular product. Most products get sealed at the site of manufacture. The FDA does have an inspection procedure in place but they do not check every single box. They look at the detail of the labels, and they look at records, they check lot numbers. The temperature records during shipping are examined closely. The FDA checks for insect and animal droppings; in some random cases, they will procure samples from containers and test the drugs. In those cases, the drugs are under quarantine and cannot be sold. If a particular company has had past issues with inspections, they can expect to have more and more batches held in quarantine. These are standard procedures," Sam said, "and products could get through if someone is looking the other way, but I can only guess."

"The problem or rather sets of problems seem to include both foreign countries and our own country," Erlich said, "I believe we can work with our own industry here, as Dr. Jones indicated, to keep a watchful eye on the production of pharmaceuticals. Jones and the FBI team have been readied to keep an active watch on all plants within our own borders. The problem seems to be outside our borders."

"Madam President, it is in our best interest and for your time as well that we get back to you with an action plan, as you requested," said Hamilton, "You may not know this, but close to 80% of our drugs active ingredients and 70% or more of our biological products are produced overseas. The supply chain for the U.S. could be targeted by terrorists if they thought to go that route.

We hope that won't happen. But now is the time to prepare. Martin and I, along with Dr. Jones and colleagues, will meet with the FDA and with your approval, the State Department. We need the ability to gain extremely close access to manufacturing facilities and their personnel within our partner countries and companies around the world."

"Thank you all. I hope you can prevent any problems before we see anything like the attacks we have witnessed within our own borders, such as occurred with the MVoneshot vaccine. And, please, let's not limit your discussion with the FDA to drugs. As I recall, we import 75% of our food, other than meat and poultry, into the country, including fish and fruit. Also, we import a large percentage of our animal products from overseas."

"Our population could be at risk in a number of ways, and this doesn't stop at the pharmacy. I need to be in direct contact with the FDA director about these issues. Let's not forget this. I expect to hear back in one week from you gentlemen on the current issue. Thank you for the critical update. I am due at another meeting." With that the President left the Oval Office, and her executive assistant brought the group out the door they entered.

The very next day the three men had a meeting set with the Secretary of State; not an easy meeting to arrange. It had been obvious that the president had prearranged the meeting with Dr.

Emily Gregson. Emily had earned her doctorate in political science at Harvard but then worked her way up slowly through the ranks in the State Department through the years. During the last Administration she had taken on the role of the United States Representative to the United Nations. Well-liked by most Western nations, she even had a flair for working with the 'evil' nations that oppose everything good in the world. Emily might have seen this as the penultimate step before a presidential candidacy of her own, but she never could see a campaign aligning with her principles. Number one, she demanded civility. And in line with civility, she expected her one-hour meeting would start on time and end on time. The CIA, FBI and Dr. Sam Jones had not yet arrived. One more minute and she would cancel the meeting.

"Dr. Gregson, your 8 AM is here," said her assistant just before 8.

"Good morning," said Emily Gregson, "I was just about thinking you were not showing," as her assistant led them into her spacious office in the Harry S. Truman Building on C Street. Elegantly designed but not overdone, her office furniture had not been anything she had chosen. In contrast, one could tell she supplied the art adorning the wall.

"Traffic," said Erlich.

Gregson gave all of them a stern look as if to say, 'You idiots, how long have you lived in Washington.'

"Please sit down," as she pointed to the sitting area and table to the left of her desk, "The president has briefed me on the issue, and now I need a little detail on what the State needs to do to assist," she said.

"Let me first just introduce Dr. Jones, from DRDG represents the Drug Research and Development Group, and of course, you know Mr. Erlich from CIA and me," said Hamilton, "What we need immediately, Dr. Gregson,

"Please call me Emily," she said.

"Yes, Ma'am. Emily. What we need immediately is tight control and oversight of manufacturing and release of all chemicals and finished products used in the final manufacture of drugs or biologics and then are sent to the United States from any foreign countries," said Hamilton.

"I would expect we already do this, no?" asked Emily.

"We do. But now we are in an emergency and critical situation," said both Jones and Erlich almost simultaneously.

"Please explain," she said, "Just one of you."

"I will," said Jones, "Typically, imports are received and reviewed randomly by the FDA. A more thorough investigation is required now. Our concern relates to the supply chain, which, as you know, is dependent on overseas suppliers for most of our products. In the case of our pharmaceutical supply, it has become very high due to concern about labor costs and doing our best to keep prices as low as possible.

"Stop Dr. Jones. Just the problem and how to rectify it," she demanded.

"Of course. My apologies.

"We spoke earlier with the President about plant inspections and monitoring employees in the Indian and Chinese generic facilities. That, in my mind, would be a good start if we get permission from these manufacturers and countries to do this."

"If I can pull this off, do you have the manpower to handle all these plants?" she asked.

"I don't think we can cover every company now; it will take a while to get up to speed, and I am not sure the FDA has the capacity to cover all these facilities either," said Dr. Jones.

"Then, why are we even talking about this as a solution," Emily asked.

"If the manufacturers and/or terrorists know we are in a country that could at least be a deterrent for an attack or an attempt on any particular drug that might be a target," Jones said.

"If that is all we have, then I will call my embassies in India and China and get things going on my end," she said, "but there is a parallel program that you need to discuss with your pharmaceutical companies here in the United States. If you recall, just last month, the President spoke about putting more people back to work. This program included people in the biotech and pharmaceutical industry, as much of this manufacturing went overseas. She spoke about the ongoing construction of new production facilities. Well, Dr. Jones, that is the no longer a backup plan. Please get the FDA and companies on board about accelerating this program. These facilities need to be built and approved. We have a potential emergency coming our way. Thank you," she said.

"I will speak to the Board and get right on it."

"Anything that you'd like to say, Mr. Erlich."

"Not at this time, thank you," he said.

"Okay, good meeting. Let us reconvene by phone in one week for an update to see what progress we've made. If there is any trouble internationally, we will get Mr. Erlich's team involved with my group sooner. Thank you again, and watch that traffic," Emily said half-jokingly.

With that, they rose from their seats. Emily walked them to the door and thought to herself that she had just met with either incompetent or overworked bureaucrats and became worried about the future more than she had been yesterday.

20

Not Him Again

April 2021

"I have nothing to say to anyone," Dr. Alan Mazer shouted, "Where are you taking me Moose?"

Moose, the straight-faced guard, led Mazer easily down the hallway to an interrogation area in the maximum-security Federal Prison in Lee County, Virginia,

"What's going on?" Mazer asked.

"Keep up," Moose ordered, "and keep it down. Do not raise your voice."

Moose had to push him into the brightly lit but starkly furnished room, containing a long table with a bench on one side and two chairs on the other. Moose placed him on the bench and cuffed both his wrists to the bar in the center of the table. Moose then left the room.

Mazer sat alone in that room for what felt like an eternity. Alan contemplated his situation. He killed his accomplice who developed and helped distribute the dangerous version of the measles vaccine. Then, he went on and tried to flee the country. Suppose he had not made these mistakes; he might never have been caught and tried for murder and terrorism. What could have been, he thought. What was going on now?

After five minutes, two men entered the room. One flashed an FBI badge, the other, in a much better-looking suit, just sat on the bench next to Mr. FBI man. They just stared at Mazer for a full 30 seconds before saying a word. Mazer felt more uncomfortable than when in the open lunch area.

"Dr. Mazer, my name is Evan Green; I am the U.S. Attorney. This is Agent Jonathan Sharp, a senior agent with the FBI," said Green, "Today, I have papers here that will explain to you that we have evidence implicating you in new criminal activity. These documents charge you with federal crimes committed against the citizens of the United States of America. It is my duty to protect the public against harm, and since you are currently in custody and incarcerated, arresting you is not an issue. But certain procedures must be followed. Do you understand?"

"No, I have rights; what am I arrested for now? I should have an attorney present, and why haven't you read me my rights," said Mazer.

"Mr. Sharp will explain in a minute; I just want to be clear that these charges relate to your collaborative efforts with insiders at Immunoviratherapeutics to change the MVoneshot measles virus vaccine…

"Wait, wait, wait, that's why I am sitting in this prison; that's what I've already been charged and convicted for," Mazer said, "you cannot charge me twice for the same crime; that's double jeopardy.

"Not quite," said Green, "It has been two years out now, and we have evidence that you placed a second 'bomb,' so to speak, in that vaccine, and people are now just getting very sick."

"I did nothing of the sort," said Mazer.

"Agent Sharp."

"Dr. Mazer, since I will be questioning you, I will not 'Mirandize' you. I have identified myself to you as a Federal agent with the FBI, and in that capacity, I do not need to advise you of your rights." As Sharp spoke Mazer looked dumbfounded.

As often as Sharp had questioned people, they did not realize that the FBI's role in protecting the entire country would be impaired if their rights were read. If subjects were advised of their rights, the Justice Department felt that important information could be held back by suspects, threats to the country would remain hidden, and 'public safety' would be at risk.

"That's fine, Mr. Sharp," said Mazer, "I will not be answering any of your questions; call me hostile or just call me smart; this is bullshit. I do not believe you. I will only speak with law enforcement with my counsel present."

"That is your right," said Sharp, "But these charges, as you see, have been filed in federal court."

"Dr. Mazer, we will provide an attorney for you at no cost after the indictment," interjected Green.

"Excellent, and I would prefer a solid pro bono attorney from a top firm in the District, not a court-appointed attorney from out here in 'Hicksville', Virgina," Mazer said.

"We will send your request to the court," Green replied.

They gave the high sign to Moose, who had been standing at the window peering into the room. He opened the door, let them out and escorted them to an exit.

A few minutes later, Moose returned to the interview area. Mazer confused to no end, waited to be returned to his cell. Moose entered the interview room, removed the cuffs off Mazer and stood him up with one giant grip on his shoulder. The large, burly guard, who in another life had played tight end for a junior college football team hoped to make it further but classes got in the way. He more or less strong-armed Mazer back down a well-lit hall to his rather dingy cell block. Mazer, at first, thought there might have been some errors in his first trial, and perhaps he was getting a lucky break.

No luck. He now knew that not to be the case. He had no idea what this new indictment was all about; a total surprise. Yes, he did conspire to modify a measles vaccine and turn it into a killer. It was a harmful product that, once injected into youths and teens, killed and maimed them. That was why he sat in this cell now…. a terrorist. But Mazer continued to wonder about these charges. The effects of the vaccine two and three years later made no sense. The virus that was changed had only acute effects he thought, nothing that could have happened now. This was crazy. Even the surviving animals injected with this strain had no long-term problems. He could not understand what happened.

He thought about what was said in the short meeting. "This will be a long and drawn-out affair. You will be arraigned, just like any other person already charged and indicted. Then you will go before a judge, but given that he was already in prison, the Federal Bureau of Prisons would manage the logistics of the proceedings. The judge and all the parties needed will come to you, Dr. Mazer," U.S. Attorney Green had said, "We won't take any chances that some parties will try to do something during transport. This will be a formality. You will not be getting out. A formality, no bail will be set. Your defense attorney has not been assigned, and he or she will make arguments for dropping the case, which no doubt will be overruled. The judge will set timelines for discovery, followed by preliminary hearings, pretrial motions, and, eventually the trial."

Many other issues came to the forefront from this vaccine debacle. Mazer was in prison for life, but hundreds of people lost jobs and fortunes, and many more could be prosecuted. The Company, Immunoviratherapeutics, had jumped the gun in distributing the vaccine. In order to show sales on record in the last quarter of the year, the sales and marketing team made a major error. Without having prior Federal Insurance, they started to sell the vaccine, in what they called a "soft" launch of the product. Just to satisfy Wall Street, the vaccine was out there on the market. But the Company was open for liability claims, without the National Vaccine Injury Compensation Program. If a defective product caused injury or death, criminal charges could potentially be brought against the Company and responsible parties.

For now, Mazer needed a defense attorney. He needed a fine and accomplished pro bono attorney. He certainly could not afford his own defense, and no one in their right mind wanted to defend this worldwide mass murderer. He was not concerned about Immunoviratherapeutics or The Baltimore medical school and University where he worked, both now dragged into the mess in separate lawsuits. The University certainly had potential huge civil liabilities to dodge since Mazer worked in their facilities. Immunoviratherapeutics died a quick death, declaring bankruptcy a year after the whole fiasco. However, individuals might still be liable for what happened at the Company.

Mazer immediately claimed his innocence. He restated that he knew nothing about the insertion of another virus into the vaccine and had been in prison for two years. How could he have been involved? Prosecution already had plenty of evidence piled up against Mazer. Plenty of circumstantial evidence existed. Labs around him at the University had worked with Bornavirus in the past. The virus was easily accessible to Mazer and was within his skill to propagate. Ashraf, the man Mazer killed and who worked on loan from Immunoviratherapeutics in his lab, could integrate the genes into the measles vaccine.

Three days later, Moose brought Mazer down that well-lit hallway again, sat him down and cuffed him to the interrogation table.

"Looks like you're getting a lawyer," said Moose, "and she's good lookin' too." Moose left the room, closed the door and went to find Dr. Mazer's counsel.

"Here you go, Ma'am, this is your client, Dr. Alan Mazer," said Moose, "I will be right outside this window. Just raise your hand if you need me." He left and closed the door.

"Good afternoon, Dr. Mazer, I am Nelle Digam, an attorney with Johnston, Howe, and MacIntosh in Washington, DC. I have taken on your case, pro bono, of course, if you are interested," she said.

"I know your firm. You also have an office in Baltimore, where I used to live and work, a very reputable firm. Are you a partner?" he asked.

"No, I have been an associate for four years. As part of our work, we take on cases like yours, or if you wish, you may seek other counsel," she replied.

"I am pleased to have you represent me, but I am confused. I am imprisoned for life times thirty. Why the additional charges, and what will this accomplish?" Mazer asked.

"Well, have you not paid attention to the outside world?"

"I have indeed," he said, "I read about the increased violence, suicides, etc., and I cannot be responsible for that."

"Well, these events have occurred in kids injected with the vaccine you altered, so either you or someone you worked with might be guilty," Ms. Digam said.

"I don't know a thing about these late events; anything I worked on would have only increased the acute effects of the altered measles vaccine. This is nonsense," said Mazer.

"This is a good start," she said, "Let's do a deep dive into that at a later date. At least you agree to work with me, and you have declared your innocence. These two steps are important for us to move forward. I also want to let you know that this criminal case is only the beginning. There could also be civil action as well."

"What? I don't have a penny left to my name, and again, I did not do anything," he said.

"I hate to break this to you, but you have done plenty. First, a civil action is ongoing against Immunoviratherapeutics related to the vaccine that was distributed and caused damage. Additional lawsuits are being filed against your employer, the Baltimore hospital and the medical organization. The action against the Company won't go anywhere since there is nothing to gain; the Company is dead and buried, but the officers are not. Additional action will most probably be brought not only against you but could also be brought against your family," she said.

"Second, a new set of civil cases will be brought forth for injury compensation related to the chronic injuries. We need to prove that you are not guilty of the set of conditions occurring now such that we remove you from liability," Digam said.

"Great, sounds to me like this is baloney. I will be spending time in court, whether I am guilty or not guilty. I am not going anywhere and do not have any resources to pay anyone," he said.

"You might not, but your family might; they might be paying for your mistakes either financially or by reputation for their whole life," she finished and waved to Moose, "I will make an appointment to see you when we have something to do. The next step will be in court, right here in prison, in front of the judge. At that time, we will have the plea-bargaining session, in which I am sure you will plead not guilty, correct?"

"Yes, of course," said Mazer.

Nelle said goodbye and thanked Moose as he opened the door. Mazer sat and contemplated his situation. Of course, he knew he was not going anywhere. But he never weighed the effects of his actions on his children or his wife. He felt he would be the only one punished for his actions if caught. Now, even his mother, who had not seen him in over a decade, suffered emotionally from the consequences of his actions.

It did not take long to arrange the next steps for Mazer's litigation issues. The Federal Bureau of Prisons handled all the logistics of the legal proceedings within the penitentiary system, so this case moved quickly because of its notoriety.

Mazer's attorney, Digam, met with him a second time, a week later, just before his second appearance in court. At that time, she told him what to expect. Having gone through this before, he remembered with clarity everything and did not look forward to a repeat of his first trial over two years ago. In his first, rather quick appearance before the judge, Mazer pleaded not guilty and promptly returned to his cell. This appearance, his second in front of the judge, was the preliminary hearing. More like a mini-trial, he knew the prosecution could begin by introducing evidence and calling witnesses, and the defense could cross-examine witnesses. But some evidence shown in the preliminary hearing could not be used in the jury trial.

The trial judge, the Honorable H.D. McCarthy, assigned to the case, entered the small courtroom on the prison premises. He was known as a judge who never wavered far from a conservative interpretation of the law and stuck with that viewpoint during his thirty-year career on the bench.

As he sat in his chair he began.

"Please be seated. I have studied this case and Dr. Mazer's prior case for which he was convicted. I have viewed the issues both in light of the law and the issues facing all attorneys and magistrates. We should all be respectful and sensitive to the time demands of our peers and all the ancillary individuals involved in these proceedings. What good would it do to go through a long and tedious court proceeding for a person who currently faces thirty life terms without parole and add on additional penalties."

"If, in fact, Dr. Mazer is responsible for the second wave of deaths or the bystander deaths due to this Bornavirus, the burden of proof will be illuminated in any civil litigation filed against not only Dr. Mazer but also in pending suits filed against

Immunoviratherapeutics executives and board members as well as the Baltimore Medical Organization. I see no reason to waste the time of everyone in this room and all the witnesses who would be called here to Virgina for a man incarcerated for life. And so, I am summarily dropping these charges against Dr. Mazer."

"Now, I have made this summary judgment, but if the Office of U.S. Attorney sees fit to appeal my ruling, that office may move to do so. Bailiff, please return Dr. Mazer to his cell immediately. Thank you all for your time. This court is adjourned."

Mazer looked at his attorney and thanked her. He knew he was not quite finished with this Bornavirus fiasco. He did not have an opportunity to prove that he was not involved. It should not have been brought against him but, it would be one of many that he would face as he rode out his life sentences in prison.

21

America Strong- Presidential Address
December 2021

President Moreno faced the cameras with a determined grit. Just a year into her term, her face and hair showed the aging of a president after a full term.

"We have come to an important nexus in our history. I am speaking with you today on several important and sensitive issues of which I have just been made aware. When I took office, I promised to involve us as a community, to address issues that we could all work on together. Today, we have reached one of those crossroads. As a nation if we address them correctly, we will carry on and thrive. I also said when I took the oath of office that I promised I would face challenges openly. Here we stand with an economy that is flat and an unemployment rate that is beginning to rise. Many blame unemployment on the influx of new immigrants who have taken jobs from U.S. citizens. I say that is nonsense."

"The unemployed are not those jumping up and down to take open jobs such as washing dishes, harvesting fruit, and cutting lawns. Now is the time that you must face the music, people; if you are sitting on an easy chair and taking in government handouts those days are coming to an end. We need all able-bodied people back to work. We are at war. This may not be a war in which you are putting on a uniform and carrying a rifle, but you will be a soldier. We need you to follow orders in the corporate world. I am instituting a brand-new initiative that will put every capable person back to work. This is not a handout. The handouts are stopping. Manufacturing is coming back home."

"Too many risks have been taken by Corporate America by placing manufacturing overseas. Yes, these risks might have given Americans less expensive products but cheaper, poorer-quality products as well. What we see is a lack of control and problems in what comes back to our shores and stores. Now we have greater problems. Remember, just a little less than three years ago, many of your children received a new measles vaccine. And you all know what happened- hundreds of deaths and sickened children. In this case, the vaccine was made right here in the USA."

"The problem was not an overseas problem. But do you know where most of our drugs and medicines are made: Overseas. Over 70% of our pharmaceuticals or active ingredients are produced overseas and shipped here. We cannot afford to have a problem with our supply chain of the products that keep us healthy. The same thing goes for our food. We import so much fresh food and food ingredients that it overwhelms our inspectors."

"So, we have a lot of work to do right here at home. We need to build more manufacturing facilities and train people to work in the plants. The FDA needs to inspect and approve hundreds of facilities quickly. I have been in discussions with the pharmaceutical and food manufacturing companies, their professional organizations and the FDA. We have a plan and this will be accomplished. The timing is very important. China is losing its workforce as they age and their younger people all want to work in technology fields."

"This program will give the U.S. an even greater economic jump worldwide. The jobs we have in the U.S. will be high-paying and will be high-tech manufacturing and scientific jobs. Construction crews are already lined up to build prefabricated large manufacturing facilities specified by the pharmaceutical companies. Not only that, our new legal immigrants are willing to work their way up, just like our ancestors did when arriving in America. There will be jobs for everyone. This is not some long-term plan. This will happen now, in the next 3 to 6 months and beyond."

"In our position as a producer nation, and not just for pharmaceuticals, our dollar will be in demand as we export more goods. Our dollar will grow stronger and remain the currency to which the world will turn. No longer will America rely on imports of products. We have the capacity and certainly the know-how to produce and export the highest quality and technologically advanced products. Together we will take the tragedy that befell us and turn it into an opportunity. America will lead the world through the 21st century. God Bless the United States of America. Thank you."

178

22

A Second Wave- The "Reverend" Kent Jensen

Spring 2022

Nari kept watch on the increasing attacks around the country and in other parts of the Western world. She surmised that these actions did not seem to be like the attacks carried out by younger people. The attacks were not unusually violent but the actions struck the chord of the American fabric of life. Taunting of various people began, and hate speech was common. Further, Nari found that no real crimes were committed.

Nari saw antisemitic behavior and actions flowing heavily, almost like a tsunami. She thought it obvious that neo-Nazi-like groups were behind the movement. Some of the more heinous activities included unknown persons leaving leaflets on all the cars in the Jewish Community Center parking lot in Westchester, NY, one day. The leaflets read, 'Today, lunch special, pulled pork or shrimp sandwiches, sauces made in Germany, 1941. Heil Hitler'. In Baltimore, on Park Heights Avenue, where at least ten synagogues were located, street crossings were painted during the night at many intersections that read 'NO JEWS ALLOWED'. She learned that yellow swastikas were painted on sidewalks on the streets in front of synagogues across suburbs in Los Angeles, Boston, and New York as the nation barely took notice of this terrifying display of antisemitism. In another coordinated attack on 65 places of worship across large and small cities alike, swastika symbols were burned with branding irons onto the front wooden doors of synagogues on a late Friday night. When members of the congregations arrived for services Saturday morning, they were overwhelmed with grief.

In the week that followed, the Anti-Defamation Organization, a group focused on education and monitoring of antisemitism worldwide, became outraged at inaction against the perpetrators of all these events. How could these events happen around the country and the world and not one soul be found? The FBI had been called in to investigate already, but no arrests had been made after several weeks of investigation. This targeting of groups involved in these activities required serious law enforcement coordination.

Nari had discovered a key component in the recent dissemination of antisemitism and bigotry. A man by the name of Kent Jensen started bringing in large crowds of people who listened to this man's hate speech. Jensen was a smooth talker. He was tall, dark and handsome, as the expression goes. He traveled the country spewing hate speech. No one knew from where he came, but his talks were evil and he did not appear to be stopping. Starting in the southwest of Arizona, in front of groups of 50 to 200 or so, his message grew viral on the internet. As he traveled first to New Mexico and then on to west Texas, Oklahoma and Mississippi, crowds grew well into the thousands. As he moved from place to place, the boots on the ground message spread… hate of everyone different- Hispanics, Blacks, Asians, and especially Jews. Jews, they ran the country.

"They run the world," he would say in all his speeches. But beyond that, the message became electronic as well. It was blasted across every social media platform by many of those who attended his "performances". Once these messages hit TikTok, Snapchat, and the rest, spewing such hate, it became absolutely impossible to quell. Social media companies could not take down the hate messages fast enough, including horrible messages of antisemitism and racism, and the messages multiplied across the net.

Lawsuits proliferated against these companies, saying free speech violations occurred under the First Amendment if messages were removed. Young people with no filters took Kent Jensen at his word, especially those kids who had no adult authority figures in their homes. Was this man molding the children of the country and the world with his hate speech? Jensen seemed to have come out of nowhere. Now the web was full of hate messages that could be traced to his preaching, yet he had nothing to do with posting any of the disgusting words and memes.

A large overlap of antisemitism and anti-Zionist hate posts had arisen on the internet now. The posts were jumbled by many of the Jensen followers, unsure of the differences. Of course, the anti-Zionist posts were usually traced to radical Islamic groups. So, the Nazi-led postings on antisemitism seemed to be in partnership with the Islamic posts. Strange bedfellows? Not really, given the alliance of the Nazis and Arab nations in World War 2.

Jensen espoused his concept based upon nothing but rehashed and old antisemitic tropes and theories proclaiming that the Jews controlled the economy. In doing so, he said, they controlled the world. The Jewish people dealt with these lies for centuries upon centuries. This was nothing new, yet it still tore into their hearts. Jensen often referred to Hitler in his talks and said that he had the final solution but didn't complete it. Nari knew he could not be stopped unless he broke the law, in which case the police could arrest him. But the Constitution allowed him free speech as long as he did not incite riots. Jensen remained clean and never broke the law. He assembled people legally and they left his speeches calmly.

If his followers broke the law, that would be another issue. But then again how can one prove a "follower" of Jensen actually participated in an unlawful act? The bigger question - where did he come from originally. Who brought him from nowhere to prominence? He had no problem obtaining money from his flock now. The FBI and JTTF had no information on this man. He was possibly a shill for another group. He came out of the blue with no background. He carried himself well but had not been questioned yet. He had not yet been linked to any crimes.

Jensen mesmerized crowds and, in a way, acted like some kind of hypnotist. Whatever he said grabbed his audience. As time went on, his speeches worsened. He never veered from his hatred and antisemitism themes, but when it came to the Jewish people, he didn't focus on Nazi Germany. He actually knew his history. He spoke about the killing of Jews in several eras, but mostly before and during the Spanish Inquisition. He knew his history.

One of his sermons would go deep into the Inquisition. 'If they were not killed, they professed to be converted to Catholicism. But hide like they might try like the Conversos of Spain did and run to foreign lands concealed as Christians, we will stop them, the Jews of America. There will be no repeat of the 15th century on our watch. Most of Mexico and South America became populated by Conversos, and many were not loyal to Christianity.'

Jensen spoke of history, the burning of temples, menacing people from their way of life, and forcing conversion to Catholicism. As a result of his speaking, Jensen developed thousands and thousands of followers and believers everywhere in the country and even beyond the border. His rallies were now outside the large cities, hidden in quiet suburbia, and in rural America. His presence on the web had just begun and was being tested. However, how Jensen communicated outside his preaching, and its impact was not yet clear. How he began, where he came from, his goals, timeline, and targets were all unclear. One thing for certain, the U.S. law enforcement agencies saw that his "flock" was all part of a homogenous group of haters.

Nari also reviewed the intelligence reports from the JTTF, the CIA, and Interpol. They all suggested that a worldwide threat of dangerous persons had also been set in place in Western Europe. Individual minor events similar to the antisemitic activities in the United States had begun in Germany, Sweden, Italy, and France. These incidents happened regularly and increased slightly in number from those typically observed. So, groups or individuals began to take action like that seen in the United States, but no zealots other than radical Muslims were out there raising havoc. No one on the order of a Kent Jensen with a traveling show was preaching around Europe. The assumption remained that the bias activities observed were not virus-related. Rather, these acts were coming from right-wing radical groups since fewer doses of vaccine were administered in Europe.

23

Evaluation of Battles from Afar
Winter 2021

The JTTF and CIA did not know how Jensen and his hate-show started and continued, but Kurt Huette and Alilah Cetin certainly did. Kurt and Alilah starting their travels from Iran, communicated with them through U.S underground personnel in the NNA (Neo-Nazi Army) through non-electronic means. Their messages could not be intercepted at this point by the robust electronic surveillance used by the FBI and CIA. Kurt commanded every action through their ground personnel. His network existed in every country they planned to visit. Only trusted persons traveled outside of Iran and carried messages to any place where attacks would be initiated. It would take longer to start, but International or U.S. authorities would not know of communications, no matter how insignificant, be it a sermon, movement of personnel, or all-out attack.

Waves of violence started suddenly, just as Kurt wished. These were seemingly separate from the shootings, cars crashing into crowds, and other large events. The one-off events, the heckling of Jews, Blacks, and LGBTQ[+] individuals, started slowly but increased in severity and numbers. Soon, these people, whoever they were, seemed to get what they wished for---news reports on all the major U.S. and international networks. Jensen became the fall guy with no proof.

The internet and all the social media outlets were blamed as well. But in fact, no link existed to Jensen. These new events were separate. This result was exactly what Kurt and Alilah hoped would occur. An upheaval where finger-pointing occurred. Everyone blamed everyone else for the huge increase in bias and bias attacks with no apparent resolution or easy way to stop the hate and no real tormentor or agitator. In the meantime, as the U.S. dealt with these issues, so did other countries, as similar attacks went on elsewhere.

In time, Kurt thought, he and Alilah might make their way to the Americas, but for now, they would be pleased to see reports of uprisings on news broadcasts. Kurt's involvement with the "Reverend" Jensen at this point would pay dividends later. Jensen, with backing from Kurt, had started a group in central Texas called Liberty Patriots. It sounded on the surface very innocent, like a positive pro-American group that any young person or veteran would be interested in and perhaps joining.

That's exactly how the group started. They went to rallies on major Federal Holidays supporting the government's action and war on terrorism. In Texas and soon throughout the Southwest, the group rode in well-organized and civil on their motorcycles, handing out flags and candy to kids on parade routes. That was coordinated with the distribution of well-conceived and artistic pamphlets for adults. Subliminal messages contained within those pamphlets and photos were sure to bring back many people to follow-up meetings.

The Liberty Patriots movement, on the surface, looked like mom-and-pop and apple pie. In actuality, the movement was a cover for a hate group, and the subliminal messages brought back the white supremacists, antisemites and anti-LGBTQ$^+$ persons the group was counting on. The new "Patriots" went to the website and saw the numerology and words used that were codes for Hitler and other heinous persons.

From there, the Liberty Patriots organization, originally started by the good Reverend, took off and was handed off to one of Kurt's generals. It then transitioned to a militaristic group that could be called upon in later times to ruffle feathers or take on larger acts of rebellion as needed. These actions were well beyond the 1940s words and actions against Jews started by Charles Lindbergh, the great aviator. He was a sympathizer of Hitler and called American Jews a danger to America because of their influence on so many aspects of industry. In fact, he developed a group called "America First", and advocated for antisemitism, befriended Hitler and clearly did not want the United States to enter World War 2.

24

The President and Judaism

April 2022

The President saw the problems, and she knew the ravings from Jensen were just the beginning. Many groups came to her and asked her to intervene, but she told them there was nothing she could do since no federal laws had yet been broken. Jewish people were the most terrorized group in the States, as they had been for years and years, but now more of the harassment took the form of physical attacks or attacks on structures.

President Moreno invited Rabbi Mattson, the Chief Rabbi of the Synagogue of Conservative Judaism, to meet with her. They had a pleasant meeting despite the topics discussed.

"It does look like all doom and gloom, Madam President," concluded Rabbi Mattson, "It always appears like that to our people. Even now computer games attack our people and our images."

"Again, thank you for spending some of your valuable time with me. I know in times like these your congregation needs you more than I do. Just in the last month, 85 synagogues received bomb threats in the U.S. alone. Thankfully, just a handful turned out to be credible and of those, only one exploded, and everyone escaped injury," said the President.

"Yes. We were fortunate. As a group, these events have continued to target our people for centuries. It has been said by greater persons than myself that it takes a courageous minority to sustain such attacks. I only hope that you, Madam President, and the rest of the good people of our country can help us sustain ourselves moving forward," said the Rabbi.

"I have promised as President to do just that. And under the increasingly severe circumstances I have witnessed just recently, with attempted attacks on houses of worship and individual signs of hate multiplying in our streets, you have my word. My law enforcement team and I will be there to protect and support you," she finished her sentence, "But hear this, Rabbi, the people of this country and the world must act to change behavior."

"I cannot raise a pen, sign my name and expect people to just change. Has that ever happened before? What can be done to change the millennia of prejudice against the Jewish people? I know that education is number one. What needs to be told is the story of the people of Israel. I know it well. The diaspora of the Israelites must be told. If you and your fellow learned rabbis can explain that the Jewish people scattered the globe 2,500 years ago, and many persons do not even know their own heritage, then maybe behavior will change."

"You know, and I know, many countries sent Jews underground to worship in hiding all over the world. In many countries, from Spain to Scotland to Russia to Mexico and elsewhere, there exist thousands of people practicing Jewish traditions, but they do not know why or what they mean. These are the crypto Jews of the world. I would bet that many of the hoodlums that are causing problems have Judaic backgrounds and do not even know it. Do you know why I am telling you this, Rabbi?"

"Madame President, I am astounded by your knowledge in this area, no, please tell me," he said.

"Of course. For my whole life, when I walked into my house, we always kissed our fingers and touched the top right side of the door jamb. I had no idea why we did this. I asked my mother and she said, we did this because my mother and my grandmother and grandfather did this in the Monterrey area of Mexico. She said after they moved to Florida before I was born, they continued to do this as well," said the President.

"My mother cleaned houses, and one person was a Jewish lady in Fort Lauderdale. My mother was curious about the bronze artwork on the door jamb and why the woman kissed it when she entered the home. The owner went on to explain that it was a Mezuzah, and inside was an important Hebrew prayer called the Shema. She told her the importance of the prayer, and displaying the

Mezuzah was an important reminder of her Jewish faith. From that time on, our family believed we must have had some Jewish lineage."

"That is a wonderful story, Madame President, and I know of many others like you who have told me similar tales. I assume you have continued your Catholic faith," asked the Rabbi.

"Yes, I have, and there are many parallels in other religions," added the President, "I have researched my family tree and have had a genetic analysis performed. As it turns out, I do indeed come from Sephardic or Spanish-Jewish descent. Many of my relatives left Spain or Portugal to avoid Crucifixion around 1500. They lived their lives as Crypto Jews in the Monterrey area of Mexico, hiding out and practicing their religion underground for several generations, never to surface as Jews," she said, "Many peoples across the world have done the same. Most of the 'Conversos', for fear of death, did convert to Catholicism and never returned to the Jewish faith. Yet, over the years, the Conversos practiced many Judaic customs but had no idea of their basis."

"We ourselves, from century to century ask why did we hide? Why did so many Jews assimilate and disappear?" asked Rabbi Mattson, "I think you have the answer."

"The history of 3,000 years of persecution shines too brightly on the answer but also on the reason to repeat our story.

And, I want you to know that our country will always be a steadfast defender of the State of Israel, where Jews have a permanent homeland."

"It has been a pleasure to speak with you; you are right. We must educate the masses. Thank you for your time, Madame President," the Rabbi exclaimed, "And one last thing, Pesach is in mid-April. You are more than welcome to join us for a seder in our home this year."

She took the Rabbi's hands, held them for a bit, thanked him and asked her assistant to guide him out of the Oval Office.

25

Bad Drug

July 2022

Radio personality Gerri Nesmith, with a late-night audience of over 3 million listeners, always gave the people what they wanted. She was a victim of a chronic neurologic disorder and tonight took to the airways as she did every late night. In an unusual show introduction for Gerri, she took on the drug manufacturers and the President, shouting out at the country's response or lack thereof, to a recent major problem:

"Before I start my show, I want to give you some news if you have not heard it yet. I cannot believe what is happening again in the good old US of A. Almost three years ago it was the devil himself, Dr. Alan Mazer, somehow inserting a bad measles virus into a good vaccine. I am pro-vaccine all the way. This guy goes and screws everything up so that people are now afraid of all the good that scientists have done. We have something even I cannot explain, and something from which we were supposed to be protected. This just in: now we have a commonly used drug, advertised on almost every evening broadcast news report, coming off the market."

"Why? Because our American pharmaceutical companies have partnered with manufacturing facilities outside the U.S. These partners are producing drugs in foreign countries. We have very little or no control over the personnel working in these plants, and that is the problem. We do not know what gets packaged in the pills and brought to our shores. So, you go to your pharmacy, put down your insurance card, pay your co-pay, or whatever, and bring home what you think is a drug made here in America. Guess what, folks…. not so."

"It most likely is made in China or India or Thailand or who knows what land. Our president, Madame Moreno, promised us that everything would be inspected. But I guess that did not apply to a foreign partner or if it did something was amiss. Ruach Pharmaceutical, a conglomerate in Israel, an excellent company, must have been targeted by a terrorist group. Its product, also sold by its American partner, MPP Pharma, just sold a drug that did not work. That drug, a widely used new product on the market for just one year, did wonders for patients with multiple sclerosis, a neurologic disease. I have this disease, ladies and gentlemen. I can't afford to take bad drugs, and neither can you."

"Now it is inactive, and patients and doctors around the world are scrambling to find active product. Instead of feeling stronger and less tingling and numbness in our limbs, patients regress, we are lethargic and depressed. A turnaround like this was not expected. Can you guess who is behind this? It is not difficult. My guess - Jihadists again. Targeting an Israeli company! They do not care if it hurts innocent people. All that matters is the hurt of Israelis and the Jewish people. Come on, this has to stop. It happened, and the timeline that the President gave to the pharmaceutical companies, along with the JTTF, the FBI, and the CIA, could not be met. Now the American people have lost faith in the Administration and in any products their doctors prescribe. Enough said for now. We can talk more about this subject later when we finish with our scheduled guests."

"Now just listen to this first. We will roll a tape from the Drug Research and Development Organization half-hour paid show on prime-time television and a town hall meeting format show. This 10-minute film 'demonstrates' the care that went into manufacturing all types of drugs and injectable and how they were checked at the border. Then we have the CEOs of many of the top companies stand with their thumbs up their you know what, and take shots from the audience and phone lines for the next twenty minutes. This is why I am losing faith…listen to these exchanges," Gerry said to her audience.

A young voice spoke up, "Thank you so much for that great film. Now how do I know that tomorrow there will not be a whole new crew of personnel filling my insulin bottles and assuring its sterility?"

"Good question. We train all our people who work in the production facilities. They all must pass certain tests before working in any area, and I am quite certain that would be true in any company, to be in compliance with Good Manufacturing Practices," said another voice.

"Yeah, great," said the young voice, "But do you know if some other person might have taken that person's place? I doubt it. No one can be monitoring everything going on all around."

'It seems to me to be a very unlikely event," an industry spokesperson said.

Gerri paused the audio.

"Ladies and Gentlemen, you cannot see the tape I am watching. You can only hear the audio feed. The young man who asked the question was whisked away by security," said Gerri, "I will put the tape back on now."

The moderator said we have another question. "Go ahead, please."

"Well, I had a different question, but I would rather follow up on that student's question. Security at overseas plants must be a big issue. How do the plant operators know if someone has been replaced or overlooked by security," she asked.

"This seems to me to be a very unlikely event," an industry executive said.

The caller said, "You said unlikely'. But even so, how did the Israeli Company or its American affiliate, MPP Pharma, have its drug, no pun intended 'doctored' and become inactive."

"I cannot answer your question. It is a one in a million event, sad to say. My colleagues and I would probably agree that this could not happen again," he turned his head, and they all barely nodded as he answered, suggesting disagreement.

"That's the end of the tape," said Gerry, "the rest of the Q and A went just as badly, and I am sure you can catch it on YouTube or elsewhere. It certainly does not help the cause of the pharmaceutical industry or their CEOs. One would have thought that they would have placed individuals with loaded questions in the audience or at least had a moderator ready to handle questions that went awry. The people were not mollified after the television appearances. My producers have told me that 'top' clips already have appeared millions of times on Instagram and TikTok to the dismay of the executives. I do hope that our Administration is working full time to fix this problem and we can talk more about this in the final hour of the show."

26

Serious Acts Begin – Stand Up

August 2022

"Hello, Sheriff's Office?"

"Yes, this is Linda. How can I help you?"

"Hi Linda this here is Jimmy Smith. I was just out on my boat fishing in Lincoln's Lake. You need to send somebody over there where the kids swing from that big tree into the lake all the time. It's bad. It's real bad."

"What's going on, Jimmy? What are you talking about?" Linda asked.

"It's bad Linda. There's a young Black person hanging from a tree. I think he's dead. No way I can get up there. Send a fire truck too. It's real bad," Jimmy said, almost crying.

"Don't try to get up there. You can get hurt. We're sending people out right now. It's good you called," Linda said, "Just stay by your boat and don't go near that big tree there. You understand?"

"Yes Ma'am. I will wait here to answer any questions the Sheriff asks, just like on TV," said Jimmy.

"Yes. Thanks again for calling, and the Sheriff said he would be there in about three minutes. Bye Jimmy," and Linda disconnected the call.

"And, did I tell you this looks like a kid …I guess she hung up. I guess I'll wait for the Sheriff now…"

Alilah and Kurt began to receive word of more sinister events occurring in the U.S., but none like the one in North Carolina. Alilah knew right away that the lynching of a young Black man would only open up wounds of racism that had just barely healed. She checked the internet and found that Menville, North Carolina, had grown to a town of 15,000 but had been established over 250 years ago.

It had seen its share of plantations and racism before the Civil War and after it as well. Up to the mid-20th century no one had ever recalled anything like this before, nothing like this at all. The local papers told stories of how the townspeople, Black and white alike, were shaken to the core. This type of racist killing of a Black member of any community had not happened anywhere in recent memory. Hate crimes did occur, but killings like this were unheard of.

The sheriff showed up with two deputy cars close behind, lights blazing, followed by a fire truck and ambulance, as well. Jimmy Smith, sitting on the ground by the side of his boat, became very excited. He had never seen this type of activity. He continued to watch from afar, afraid to move any closer than the lakeside. After one of the EMTs climbed up on the limb and determined that the young man had died, the firetruck pulled up, raised a ladder, and one man climbed up. He carefully untied the noose around his neck and brought him down. None of the men in the unit recognized him. The Sheriff then called Jimmy over to the area.

"Jimmy, do you know this person," he asked.

"No sir, I have never seen him, never." Jimmy said, "If he was from town, we'd know him, and if he lived on the lake, I'd know him."

"Did you see anybody else around here," asked the Sheriff.

"I was fishing at the big bend on the lake all morning. I just came around the corner after lunch. I did not see nobody. I called Linda as soon as I saw him dangling there. I was scared," he said, shaking.

"There is no reason to be scared now. Whoever did this is gone, and we are here. We will get them. See these tire tracks," said the Sheriff, "Not too many people around here have brand new tires or large vehicles. That's a start. We will find them."

The EMTs took the body back to the small community hospital in town, and the deputies and Sheriff looked more carefully at the site of the hanging after everyone else cleared out. Jimmy took his boat and continued his fishing. He seemed relieved that the local law enforcement had things under control. They searched around for the better part of an hour and discovered nothing but some fibers of rope used in the hanging of the young teenager. The only information they had were the tire tracks and their depths and widths; nothing else to go on for now. It might be possible that an autopsy would give some additional clues.

Alilah continued to read reports online. In a matter of hours, the internet news and social media outlets buzzed about the African American teen found hanged by the lake. This information sparked rage but not fighting between races, the people were calmer and smarter, at least locally. Most thought this incident was, in all likelihood, sparked by the mad cries of the Reverend Jensen. He spouted hate for anyone who did not look like him or did not believe in "his God".

Despite the President's warnings in her recent address, thousands followed the Reverend Jensen, and thousands were now militaristic in their beliefs. He brought the country back 150 years or more. What could this town do or communicate to the rest of the nation? A plan from a small town in North Carolina would be a start. No one in the Federal Government had tried a thing, and doing nothing obviously did not work.

As she sat by her computer and Kurt napped, she wondered about her role. It was always about global Intifada and her long-term goal- a safe and equitable home for Palestinians. Now she was involved with a Nazi whose goal was to take over the world. Then, suddenly, Alilah saw another news item from the day before. Overshadowed by the hanging in North Carolina, she felt a pang in her gut and heart. A bombing occurred in a playground outside an elementary school in Malden, Massachusetts. Alilah knew her children could now be in danger as well. Malden was just two towns over from Revere and had a large population of immigrants. She wondered if the explosion, which the report said injured many children on the playground, was carried out by NNA. She thought if it was time to reanalyze her role and future with Kurt.

As news spread, so did fear in the suburban area of in the Research Triangle Park area. How could something like this occur in 21st-century America. The lingering Old South was rekindled from the few remaining embers by shrewd racists. High-tech or otherwise, in this area of the country, some people could be influenced by snake oil salesmen. The Old South could erupt.

Thankfully, knowledgeable people understood they could not stay confined to their homes nor keep their children within the walls of their houses. They read the accounts from the Holocaust when millions of Jews were rounded up and forced into the smallest of quarters and then barely given enough to sustain their lives each day. They had little hope for survival. It would have been a death sentence to attempt to fight their captors. With little sustenance, they died or were murdered quickly if they could not provide the labor required in the concentration camps.

Here in America, people still had choices. The gangs of criminals, or whoever they were, could not confine people and stand up to the organized strength of whole towns. Now was the time to fight back against these bigots and racists. The leaders within towns started to get the word out that the bias and hate activities could not persist. Savages without authority would not lead, harass, and terrorize good citizens. This activity must stop.

This message came initially from Menville, the small town where the lynching occurred. Now known because of the event, posting of that hanging was repeated by the millions on every conceivable social media outlet in the world. Soon, Menville sent messages many times a day about hate and the people who retransmitted it. This town stood up against hate. Citizen patrol groups, unarmed, stopped strangers from entering their towns and required them to state their business and show identification.

A peace started to develop, and the town shared its methodology with the country online. These people were not hicks, despite the fact that Jimmy, one of the few unfortunate and undereducated people in the area, found the hanged teenager. Most people in the town were highly educated and skilled workers. Soon the methodology of citizen oversight of towns and small cities began not only in neighboring locales in the Carolinas but in many other States as well. The people had started to see or suspect the same issues in their own home towns as the ones that Reverend Jensen had passed through with his cronies. The locals worked with authorities as volunteers to ensure that their towns would not be invaded by hate groups. Halting all strangers passing on through could not be a long-term solution, but it was a start for this and other small towns.

Alilah read the speech from a Menville leader, "We will not be quivering animals hiding in our little hovels. If we continue to hide, we lose our identities and distinction. We are humans and cannot lose our dignity. Who says that these racist and antisemitic, antisocial pigs will take away our freedoms. The President has told us we must take charge and stand up for ourselves. First, extremist Islam terrorists hit us and our country, and the world has not been the same for over twenty years. Now the racial, religious and social bias of the past has returned and, worse yet, exploded right here to the surface without any apparent repercussions. We as a people cannot let this continue. Whoever leads these hate mongers must be off the streets. These haters cannot live in our society unpunished."

She thought that speech would be trouble. The message was recorded by a local town reporter and sent as a press release and an update related to the hanging. Also repeated millions of times on social media and on television coverage, it became a mantra for many Americans and started a movement around the world as well: Stand up for yourself, your neighbor and your country.

With that, small groups in towns and burbs around the country began to meet spontaneously. It mattered not whether these individuals were white, Asian, Black, Hispanic, Jew, Muslim, Christian or Whatever. They started to meet and understand that something and someone had turned the country around. The man from Menville had put his finger on the problem. They cannot hide and submit to an unknown group of racists. In general, as a country the people had worked well together, and that had been the case for the last sixty years since the end of World War 2. It had only been during the last twenty years that they had become a nation divided. How had this happened?

27

Mirror Mirror On The Wall - You're Killing Me

May 2022

Emily Gregson, Martin Erlich, and Jonas Hamilton waited anxiously in an anteroom to the Oval Office. Major problems brewed, and the fires burned. The three of them were here to meet with the President for one reason only, to put them out.

"She is ready for you, go ahead in," said the President's assistant.

Before they barely sat on the sofas, the President started to speak.

"I thought I gave our top persons in this country plenty of time to work out any potential issues," President Moreno said, "Now we have another disaster coming across our borders. First, the Israeli drug was targeted; now a generic."

"At this point all we can do is search and seize whatever we can; this fake pharmaceutical is as good as it gets and passed all the inspection at the border," said Jonas Hamilton, FBI Director, "It comes down to our rules and regulations. The FDA states that an approved product that is imported must have the same appearance, shape, color, imprint and scoring and must be made by the same methods and conform to the same specifications as in the approved license or New Drug Application."

"From what I understand, most of the L-dopa is made by this one company in India and packaged and sold by several generic firms around the world, correct?" asked the President.

"Yes, that is correct. L-dopa has been used for years for treating Parkinson's Disease. How could the mirror image drug, D-dopa, slip in," asked Emily Gregson, Secretary of State, "This mirror image drug is not only ineffective in treating Parkinson's. It is killing people. It is wiping out key white blood cells; these people get something called granulocytopenia. Many people, especially older people, cannot fight off infections before it has been determined that patients received this ineffective product."

"Could someone explain to me what this mirror image thing is all about; my earth science in college did not cover this, and if it did, it's long gone from my memory banks," said the President.

"I am not a chemist," said Emily, "but from what I understand, atoms in the molecule that make up the drug can be flipped around. These mirror images are called enantiomers and will look identical to the real, active molecule but may be inactive or have totally different activities. There are many examples.

Thalidomide comes to mind as a horrible example. The D-version of the molecule came on the market initially for anxiety in the late 50's and then was found in the 60's to cause horrible birth defects in the babies of mothers who took the drug for morning sickness. Thirty years later, the other version of the molecule, the L-form, stimulated the immune system and blocked blood vessels from forming around tumor tissue. L-Thalidomide, the mirror image version, became a new cancer therapeutic."

"Emily, thank you. So, L-dopa does the job and D-dopa does damage, wiping out white blood cells. Geez, I cannot imagine what will hit us next. Just eight months ago, we had the top pharmaceutical chief executives and representatives from their manufacturer's organization in this office. We gave them six months to address the biggest concern we all had. Now we sit here on our hands, and it's eight months later. Director Hamilton, you are telling me that innocent people who are already fighting Parkinson's disease are now receiving a drug that does not work. This is over the top. We cannot assure our country that anything manufactured overseas coming into our country is the real thing as if it were made in our own backyard," said President Moreno, "This is a major disaster for the current patients and for anyone else who is going to take that next pill that is coming in from overseas; do you have an answer or any confidence whatsoever?"

"I am embarrassed…

"Embarrassed is the last word to use, Director Hamilton," the President interrupted, "What am I supposed to do? I do not care one iota about politics here. I need this fixed. I have a responsibility for almost 340 million people in our country; the next time one of them goes to the pharmacy, I do not want them to get a death sentence. What we need to do right now is speak to the top medical people in and out of the government and then get and give some wise counsel to the people of our nation. Director, you mentioned all the testing required before a drug is released. How can this, a mirror image drug, be released, pray tell."

"We can only assume that the work of companies in our allied countries in evaluating employees at overseas manufacturing facilities did not meet our standards. We must force the issue going forward, and I do see that as a national and international priority given the problems that have occurred with two drugs now," said Hamilton

"Director Hamilton, I expect you to convene with the FDA Director and get this moving; do not spare any time. I want inspectors permanently placed in all the generic plants around the globe in four weeks' time; you will have to work with Emily on this to smooth things over with the various countries," the President demanded, "There should be no hesitancy given by our pharmaceutical or biotechnology companies given the looming drug safety issues."

"Martin, I have not heard one word from you. Are you mute today?"

"No, Madam President, the Agency will assist the FBI and the Secretary in any way we can globally," said Erlich.

The President took a deep breath and started to leave the Oval Office. She turned to them both and said, "Don't wait four weeks if things are going south. Get Sam Jones, the head of the Drug Research and Development Group, lined up. I want all these generic drugs and pills made here, right back home in the U.S. I said this in our first meeting, and I am damn serious about it." She left the room.

Emily led the group out of the Oval Office.

"I would like to meet with both of you and whoever you think will be needed in the room at 3 PM today at CIA headquarters. Will that work for you?'"

"I will summon my CIA colleagues and clear out a conference room and virtual conference area. 3 PM sharp," said Erlich.

"Perfect. I will have an agenda and will invite the FDA Director to join us," said Emily, "see you all at 3 PM."

With that, they left the White House for their respective power bases.

28

Leaving for India and Beyond

December 2021

Kurt said, "Alilah, this can be a slow and tortuous route to Bangalore, India. It will be nothing like our visit to Saudi Arabia."

"I understood from the very beginning that our mission would not be easy," she said.

After a week on the sea and road, Kurt received disturbing news from the United States. He heard word that Reverend Jensen's overused hardline preaching tactics and the ill-placed militias started to have limited effects. Further, resistance began to increase. Jensen's people could not enter certain areas as easily as in the past. Many towns and people fought back against him and his followers, blocking entrances to their communities. Kurt felt so irritated that such strong opposition developed against the Jensen "forces". They could not make further headway or initiate disruptions without exposing themselves.

Kurt and Alilah did not want to go to North America now. Jensen, only one of Kurt's tactics, needed to be toned down or relieved of his duties and soon. Kurt thought a reboot or some sort of encouragement from him could very well change the trajectory of these early battles for supremacy. Middle East and European tactics continued to work well, but in America, it appeared that his own inattention to local management resulted in poor results. He needed to be on site. And, the only thought now was whether they should both risk the trip to North America. A poor decision now could negate decades of Kurt's planning. If they traveled separately, he thought, they could accomplish many more goals, meeting with many field generals and planning attacks for the future. He made his decision as risky as it might have been.

"I know you well enough to see that you are deep in thought. I have to ask you," said Alilah, "We just traveled from Riyadh. Now we have arrived in India. How do your worldwide minions have such loyalty to you without even knowing or meeting you?"

"Much of the loyalty has been generational. I am happy to have inherited it and will explain this to you shortly. And on top of that I am lucky enough to repay my loyal followers not only with praise but wealth beyond their wildest dreams. This keeps them loyal to me and, of course, to our cause," Kurt replied.

As Kurt promised, they spent several busy days before leaving India, meeting with insiders at two giant generic pharmaceutical manufacturers in Bangalore. They conspired with Kurt and the NNA previously. Even though travel to the U.S. was needed immediately, this part of their overarching plan could not be overlooked. Reports so far indicated that their work had gone well, and modified drugs entered into the pipeline and caused major problems in developed countries. Their hopes were to expand these operations. So far, at least two drugs manufactured for major worldwide companies had been compromised. The drugs were distributed before detection by regulatory authorities and caused havoc.

Another new terror tactic is exactly what Kurt and his co-conspirators around the globe planned and hoped for in a long series of activities. It was a tactic that would go well beyond his supremacist battle activities and, if played correctly, would accelerate the "evolutionary" theory. The weak and sick would die quickly, much faster than in any Darwinian world. Only the strong survived in Kurt's ruthless world, and only certain strong people at the ready would remain.

After the meetings with the pharmaceutical manufacturers, Kurt spoke, and Alilah listened intently with a new group of trusted food ingredient producers for activities at a later date. Kurt wished to be ready for new and alternate plans, as all great commanders must do.

Kurt felt it was time to move on from India, with the troubles caused by Jensen in the States. Traveling anonymously in India for anyone became more difficult with each passing year. He knew that security and border control was tighter with each conflict in the East. India became more and more cautious as to the persons it let in and out of its country. Despite their perfectly forged passports and other identifications required for worldwide travel, Kurt and Alilah could not afford detection by any authorities. Kurt had not traveled far from Asia, but Alilah, who recently went around the world, needed to take extreme caution at all ports of exit and entry.

Kurt, well aware that India imported oil from several countries seized on a new opportunity. A West African ship had just been reported to be due to unload crude oil at Cochin in the south of India. Based on this information, the two masterminds headed for Cochin, a relatively small port, to bribe their way onto this ship. This could give them a head start westward. From Africa, travel would get even more difficult, but private air passage would not be out of the question.

After leaving their used BMW on a side street in a not-so-great location, Kurt and Alilah headed on foot toward the port. The car was an expense and just one of several fine vehicles "donated" to the local economies when Kurt needed to travel without a driver.

Kurt felt good. He saw the tanker ship in port. He queried a dock worker and determined that the ship had just arrived the night before and fuel had not yet been totally offloaded. Alilah and Kurt now had time to find the right contacts to attempt to board the empty ship headed back to West Africa.

A quick stop at a cafe for local cuisine not only fit into their schedule after the long trek from Bangalore but was also a necessity. Both of them were both exhausted and famished. Thankfully, for a tea-drinking country, India had more recently developed a taste for strong coffee and grew some of the best in the world. Kurt and Alilah needed plenty of caffeine to start the day as neither had slept other than an hour or so at a rest stop on the road.

"The coffee is great here," said Alilah.

"I cannot wait to eat," said Kurt.

They both ordered quickly, Kurt giving Alilah recommendations as he had cooked Indian food at home often. Kurt ordered a rice-based dish, poha filled with nuts and Alilah got a high protein-packed breakfast dish, moong dai chilla, just in case she'd be required to work on that ship.

After their leisurely breakfast, they continued their walk to the port. Kurt checked a list of ships online and their captains. He was well prepared. Kurt intended to speak with the harbor master about the Maltese-flagged ship, The Antarctica, and its next destination, after it completed unloading its fuel.

A ten-minute walk brought Kurt to the harbor offices. Alilah stayed outside on a bench by the water, just watching pelicans dive into shallow waters for easy prey. Very little human activity could be seen. Almost everything ongoing was automated.

Inside, the Harbormaster looked quizzically at Kurt as he introduced himself.

"Mr. Huette, it is quite unusual for someone to walk in off the street and ask to see or speak to the captain of a commercial vessel," said Mr. Gupta, the Harbormaster.

"I am sure it is Mr. Gupta," Kurt replied smoothly, "In this case, it is of extreme importance that I see him, Captain Forrest. We have a mutual connection in Senegal, of which he is not aware. We are both in this person's will and we need to visit this person together and soon."

"Well, I am not sure why this urgency, but I imagine it must be important."

Kurt interrupted Gupta, "Oh, sir, it is. I expect this person might pass in the next couple of months, and she would like proof of life now and to speak with both of us very soon. I really need to get aboard the ship and speak with Captain Forrest before he leaves."

"I will arrange this for you," pointing outside, he asked, "is that your wife sitting on the bench out there?"

"She is my traveling companion, Ms. Cetin, waiting patiently for me," Kurt replied.

"I will call you; what is your number?"

"My phone battery is low. I will return here in an hour, and if you do not yet have an answer at that time, my phone should be sufficiently charged by then," Kurt said.

"See you then," said the Harbormaster.

"Thank you very much, sir." And Kurt exited the small office, heading toward Alilah.

"Let's walk away from this area," Kurt said, "I gave the Harbormaster, Mr. Gupta a story that the captain of that ship and I need to meet about an important legal matter.

"What possible matter could you have fabricated that a Captain of some tanker and you have in common," Alilah said, almost laughing as they turned up a side street toward some shops just opening.

"Simply this, the captain and I are both listed on the will of a wealthy woman in Senegal. She wants to see of us very soon and meet with us before she makes any final amendments to her will. I do not know any other ties to Captain Forrest," Kurt responded,

"Based upon this I will try to appeal to his good nature, I hope, for us to get passage to Dakar, the port in Senegal."

"Let's hope this works, Kurt; otherwise, we might be stuck in this port city for who knows how long. I expect there aren't many other ways we can get out of this place," she said.

After an hour of apparent browsing and shopping, going in and out of small shops and purchasing nothing, they headed back to the harbor office to see Mr. Gupta. He had just hung up the phone after speaking to Captain Forrest on the bridge of the ship. The crew and ground personnel had completed the transfer of the crude oil, and the ship would begin its return voyage to West Africa the next morning at daybreak.

"Hello again, Mr. Huette, and this must be Ms. Cetin, your travel companion. Nice to make your acquaintance," said Gupta.

"Thank you, the pleasure is mine," Alilah said.

Kurt interrupted the banter, "So Mr. Gupta, does the captain have time to see me about this important matter."

"Yes, Captain Forrest will see you straight away. Both of you have permission to board the ship. The captain awaits you, and from my brief conversation with him, he has some news for you as well," said Mr. Gupta.

Kurt tried to look undisturbed but did raise his brow a bit. He had made up this whole story, so what was Forrest telling Gupta.

"Mr. Gupta, thank you for all your help. I guess we will head over to the ship and board now. Thank you again."

"You are welcome. Good luck," said Gupta.

With that, Kurt and Alilah did an about-face, looked at each other with a tight little smile, and headed to the pier where The Antarctica was tied up. This was the ship on which they hoped to "hitch a ride" to Africa. Upon boarding the tanker, the two leaders of the NNA were brought quickly to see Captain Forrest. He stood proudly on the bridge giving orders to several individuals as they prepared the ship for the return voyage to the next port to take on more crude oil. As he was introduced to his guests, they immediately took leave to a private area just behind the control room. They all sat around a small table, and the captain smiled.

"I finally have the pleasure to meet my commander-in-chief," said Phillip Forrest, "and this must be Ms. Cetin."

"What do you mean?" said Kurt.

"I am one of your secret sailors; you do not have much of a navy, but you have a few NNA occult ships. The Antarctica is one of them," he said.

Kurt stood up, gave Phillip a hug and exclaimed, "How do you know who I am or what I look like? This seems unreal and honestly, I am perplexed and concerned about the leaking of my identity. Do not get me wrong. I am pleased to have allies and strength around the world."

"Of course I know your name; you are our leader, and I understand your apprehension. Do not worry," Phillip said, "Your name is known to only a few of your generals and naval captains in the world, as you know, one on each continent and your navy. After today, we will use new papers for your travels. Your picture has never surfaced. I only picked up your name from the Harbormaster."

"Well, we hope you can take us to the west, to Senegal. We now need to get to North America to meet with some of the generals to discuss strategic changes," said Kurt, "Our work is going well in Europe and Asia, but we need new direction and to make some alterations in the States."

"It will be my pleasure, sir," said Captain Forrest, "I will treat you to a fine meal tonight on land, and then we will ship out tomorrow. We have excellent quarters for you and Ms. Cetin."

"I want to thank you for being here for us, although I know it is quite fortuitous," said Alilah.

"What a pleasure to have found a comrade in arms," Kurt replied, "We look forward to our voyage together."

After about a week at sea, many of which were rough days on the water, the three NNA members met again in the captain's quarters. Captain Forrest wished to review plans and discuss recommendations on the continuation of the voyage.

"It is in your best interest that we modify our trip a bit," said the captain, "You do know that it typically takes us thirty days without any problems at sea to get all the way to Dakar."

"That is a long haul to Senegal," said Kurt and Alilah almost simultaneously.

"Yes, we must pass through the Suez Canal and then across the Mediterranean Sea before getting through the Straits of Gibraltar. Now if you agree, my plan has changed. I intend to pull into port in Algiers and stop for some unscheduled work on the ship for a day. At that time, you should disembark, never to be seen by me or my crew. This shortens your trip immensely. Otherwise, you will be heading too far west and south with us to the west coast of Africa. In Algiers, you can catch a flight to Paris and then onto the U.S. or Canada," he said, "And you can still use the papers and passports that we prepared for you and Alilah showing your home as Senegal."

"My goodness, you have planned this out quite well. Maybe you have done this previously," scoffed Kurt.

"No, I play chess, and I play it well. And I want my commander to be ahead of the game as well," said Phillip, "Besides, I am guessing that Alilah wants no more of the high seas, and the only good way out of Dakar would have been a long luxury cruise."

"Oh please, no. Thank you for your forward-thinking," Alilah said, as she stood up and kissed the captain on the cheek.

In just a matter of days, they departed The Antarctica without any issue, and Alilah could not have been more pleased to be off that tanker. She had her sea legs but was happy to be on solid ground after twenty days at sea. As she walked with Kurt to get a car to the airport, he took her hand. She looked like a drunken sailor, felt like she was still on the ship, and had difficulty walking unassisted. She only worried she might not be allowed to board an aircraft.

Flying to Paris was no problem from Algiers, but onto North America, they both thought could be an issue. They decided to risk the trip but decided it best to take different flights. Kurt took a direct flight to Newark from Paris. Alilah opted to fly to Toronto and then find a way south from there instead of flying directly to the States. Although over two years had passed since she escaped as Sabina Mazer, reducing the risk was a wise decision.

Kurt had never ventured to the U.S. and expected not to have any problem entering the country. As anticipated, he boarded his flight with no problem whatsoever. Alilah headed to her home "hemisphere "with papers from Turkey. She had undergone multiple name changes as well as physical and cosmetic alterations since leaving the States. Her body composition and musculature changed, and she became so much darker, having been in the sun constantly.

Her hair was now extremely short, but that really did not matter, as it was covered by her hijab, as were her eyes, nose and almost all of her cheeks. She thought she did not have to worry about being caught as the former Sabina Mazer. But Alilah always felt torn between her duties and loyalty to Kurt and the love that she still harbored for her children and her parents as well; that love could bring her down at any time. Might she change plans and head home? This thought nagged at her despite the devotion she had to her cause and not necessarily Kurt's devotion to worldwide domination.

29

Kurt Makes it to New Jersey

2022

Kurt did not enjoy his first trans-Atlantic flight. His plane to Newark encountered strong headwinds, and his flight took close to 8 hours to cross the Atlantic. With the sun up all day during the flight and most of the window curtains not drawn, Kurt felt exhausted. He did not get much sleep during the long, bright day. As the plane landed, he focused on two things: did Alilah get on her flight, and where could he now get some rest. Back in Paris, where the flight originated, it was close to 9:30 PM. Kurt, now traveling as Henrik Josephs, since boarding the flight in Paris, felt confident in his ability to transit through passport control.

He was correct. He showed his papers and easily walked through immigration control. He had just a carry-on bag and briefcase and was waved right through customs. As soon as he passed outside the Newark airport, he called Alilah's phone. Her plane departed ninety minutes before his and was scheduled to land in Toronto before his plane arrived in Newark. No answer. He called again and let it go to voice mail.

She might have dumped hers for some reason. Kurt, currently "Henrik Josephs", decided to take a taxi to downtown New

York. Having never been to the most famous city in the world, he felt a need to go there. He found a room at the Marriott on Broadway near Times Square and just decided to stay there. He was both excited and exhausted at the same time. Hoping to connect with Alilah, he tried her phone one more time. Again, there was no answer. He tried to sleep but even though over tired from the long trip, his worry for her whereabouts kept him wide awake.

Kurt did not have true romantic feelings for her, but he was grooming Alilah to be the next in line to command his army. For now, she remained his number one concern. He also believed that she might be able to continue his bloodline. They never discussed this possibility, but he planned to broach the subject with her on this trip. Without her, it was likely that the Hitler lineage would end without her help. Kurt had never had a relationship with a woman for as long as he had with Alilah. She might be willing to carry his child.

He brought himself back to the present. He thought back to the flights in Paris. Did she make it on the plane? Did she have problems upon arrival in Toronto? If so, her phone might have been confiscated. He tried ringing one more time; again, no answer. That was it. No more calls from this phone, he thought or from this location. He immediately decided to leave the hotel.

He grabbed his few possessions and took the next elevator down to check out. He next headed to the concierge area. Walking to the concierge desk, "Henrik" asked for the best transportation to Newark Airport.

"Sir, I can call a car or taxi, but at this time of day, your best bet is public transportation. The traffic now is very heavy crossing the river and needs to be avoided."

"Thank you; where is the bus?" said Henrik.

"No sir, the busses are a problem as well; you should walk to 42nd Street and 7th Avenue and then take the subway to Penn Station," said the concierge, as he pointed the directions to walk, "From there, you can find either a New Jersey Transit train to Newark Penn Station or a direct Amtrak train to the Airport. I hope that helps."

"Yes, thank you so much," and Henrik handed him a five-dollar bill as he scurried out the door, without checking out.

In Paris, a young woman named Darcy Allard took a motorcycle into the countryside for a long ride. She stayed in a nice apartment on the left bank off the Seine for the last few days. Old friends from high school days came in handy, especially when hiding out in foreign countries. These two friends had originally met years ago at an undisclosed location in the Middle East. They had trained for a common cause and kept in contact infrequently.

Now "Darcy" needed some fresh air outside the city. Darcy felt such a time could well be worth the break to sort things out after having spent the two years of her life training and planning for the great worldwide Intifada, along with a Nazi takeover of the world with Kurt Huette. Darcy had no interest in running the world or the new Nazi regime that Kurt Huette envisioned.

Her goals and those engrained from her teen years focused on more specific ideals - the fatwa originally proclaimed by Ayatollah Ali Khamenei in 2012 that all Jews worldwide must be destroyed. She understood the fatwa further clarified the need for the destruction of Israel, as its nuclear capability demonstrated a great threat to Iran.

Now, she needed to figure out her next steps; Darcy had finished her work with Kurt but not her original plans of a global Intifada and war against the United States. Not a lone wolf but also not working with ISIS or al-Qaeda, Alilah needed a place to plan the future and somehow contact her prior confederates to get back to their goals.

Drinking her second glass of wine at a local bed and breakfast and watching the sunset over a small vineyard, Darcy relaxed for what felt like the first time in years. She still had huge goals and knew with hard and determined work, they could be attained. But sitting alone just once in so long without any worldwide cares, crises, training or running felt better than anything she could imagine and gave her pause. Darcy knew in the end; she would have to get back to work. Now, she, at this time actually had a feeling of elation as she watched the sun start to dip over the vineyard. Seeing beauty and not thinking of war or killing for just a moment felt good in her heart. How could she differentiate these warm feelings from those destructive thoughts and actions of killing a whole population. Of course, she had performed the wonder and miracle of giving life to her twins, but now she had made the difficult decision to leave them behind and put them aside; they were secondary to the larger goals of the Intifada. It was painful, but she made that choice for her people.

She knew now, as a Muslim, why she should not partake in alcohol. It made her second guess her real objectives. She dumped out the remainder of the wine on the grass under her table and walked into the bed and breakfast, disgusted with herself for thinking like she had.

At dinner that evening, Darcy finalized her plans. She would ride back to Paris in the morning and spend a day or two with her real friend, Alice, before heading back to Algiers. Kurt provided her with sufficient resources to move forward with his plans if anything happened to him. Darcy had no idea what became of him after entering the United States, and at this point she really did not care. For all she knew, he continued with plans to meet with his field generals in the States, and he assumed that she had been detained. In any case, Darcy restarted her own mission now and would use his funds for the benefit of her cause, irrespective of Kurt's new Nazi regime.

She would have no problem returning to Algeria, the country from where she arrived the week before. Darcy also knew that Algeria, an Islamic country, contained many allies to her cause, including Al-Qaeda in the Lands of the Islamic Maghreb and AQIM, an Islamic militant organization. She felt there could be no better place to reinitiate her efforts for a militant Islamic Jihad and redevelop her plans for the global Intifada.

30

Henrik Reaches Out Too Far

2022

Henrik arrived at Penn Station and then threw his phone in a waste bin. He headed down the stairs from the subway track, seeing the dominating large board in the center of the hall listing all the trains entering and exiting Penn Station. The numbers changed continuously as he looked at the screen, confusing him and apparently others. He noticed that one Amtrak train would be leaving for Newark International Airport in ten minutes. He was not quite sure of his plans or where to go. Maybe he should fly to Toronto or even Paris to find Alilah?

He once again thought about his family legacy. Now, he wondered why he had not spoken to Alilah previously about having children with her. He knew now he should have been open with her about his desires and wishes. Should he go to the airport, buy a new phone and see if she answers? After that, he could leave directly from Newark or at least coordinate his next steps depending on whether or not she is in communication.

He ran to the ticket counter and waited behind two other customers while the clock ticked. Finally, he bought a ticket, with less than three minutes to spare, and ran down the stairs to the

Amtrak train track for the airport. He made it onto a car just before the train doors closed.

During the short twenty-minute trip to Newark, Henrik thought his best chance of finding Alilah would be flying to Toronto and trailing her from there. Upon arrival in Newark, he boarded the Airport Rail Line and got off at Terminal A, from where Air Canada flights departed.

Henrik Josephs approached the ticket counter with his credit card and passport to buy a one-way ticket on the next flight to Toronto. Three things in particular caught the attention of the veteran ticket agent. She had worked in this industry for quite some time and noticed on his passport stamp that Mr. Josephs had only arrived in the States, right here in Newark, through immigration less than 5 hours ago. Second, he planned to purchase a one-way tickct, and third was travelling without baggage and had arrived from Paris earlier. All of these things did not seem to make too much sense, especially since this man had used these travel documents just one time. A new traveler at his age she questioned herself.

"So, the next flight leaves in one hour; I have one business class seat available, an aisle, or I can put you in any number of coach class seats," said the ticket agent.

"Let's go with the coach seat. It is just a short flight, correct?" asked Henrik.

"Yes, it is a little over an hour as scheduled; would you prefer an aisle or window seat?" she said.

"I would like a window seat, thank you,"

"Very well, with tax and fees, that will be $248.00 for your one-way ticket to Toronto."

Henrik handed his charge card to her and watched as the transaction went through smoothly. He finally had a sense of calmness.

As the ticketing process continued, the agent notified security of a possible issue. She had sent a photograph from the camera on her computer to the central security area. This ensured that this person would undergo specific questioning and extra screening before being allowed to exit the country.

She handed Henrik the ticket in a paper jacket and indicated the direction of the security check-in and gate number. "Thank you for flying with Air Canada," she said. "And thank you for your courteous and prompt service," said Henrik, and he quickly moved toward security and his gate area.

31

The Next Step

2022

Her first mistake may have been making a call overseas to the Imam in Baltimore. Darcy needed a contact person in Algeria to extend her now life's work of continuing her plan for global or worldwide Intifada. She also needed a huge favor from the Imam. She did not think that a brief call on a satellite phone could be traced but could not be absolutely sure. In any case, she made the call.

"Hello," said the Imam, woken from a dead sleep.

"I apologize for waking you. I know it is very early in the morning, this is Sabina," she said.

"As-Salam-u-Alaikum, Praise Allah. You are alive," said her Imam.

"Yes, and I have just a minute or two to speak. My phone may be traced. Kurt Huette must be stopped. His goals are not our goals. He has just travelled to New York, and I am sure he will be leaving shortly for Toronto to look for me. That is all I can say. Stop him. Please give his name to Canadian and U.S. authorities, anonymously of course. Tell them his plans include escalating deadly race and bias attacks, continuing to poison the worldwide pharmaceutical supply, and increasingly influencing Americans with right-wing hate speech. We will continue our own agenda soon enough without him. I must hang up. Thank you, my friend," and with that, Sabina, aka Alilah, now Darcy, ended her phone connection with the Imam.

She hoped her message and favor were received clearly so early in the morning and would be handled. She now knew that her next stop would be Annaba, a large seaport on the northeastern coast of Algeria. Darcy did not know into what types of danger she may be heading. Annaba, despite its beauty on the Mediterranean coast, was known for its high level of crime, kidnappings, political unrest, and terrorist activities. She would have to find her contact person in this dark yet exquisite-looking city.

Darcy's roommate and companion, Alice, and not the fictitious Alice Germain, from years past, took her to de Gaulle airport for her trip to Algeria.

"Sabina, or Darcy, my friend, whatever name you are using these days, I just want you to know that you are safe with me anytime you come to Paris. And the sat phone you used has two modes. I turned the GPS mode off. It was not traceable when you made your call to whomever. You need to become more tech-savvy in the twenty-first century. You do not have to worry," Alice said.

"You do not know how relieved I feel now," said Alilah, "I only wish you had told me earlier. And, my name is now Alilah, Alilah Cetin, as it has been for the last two years."

"I apologize," said Alice, "I didn't think about it until just now. Forgive me, and remember you have a safe haven here, my dear friend. And keep the phone, Alilah. You will need it as you continue your battles."

"Thank you, thank you," said Alilah, "I will repay you. You know I will."

"Repayment will be made when our goals are reached. Do not worry," Alice responded.

As they arrived at the airport, both jumped out of the car and hugged each other at the departure area. They hoped that not so many years would pass between the next meeting as they said their farewells. But the two of them shed tears as each knew that this could be the last time they ever see each other again.

Alilah felt relaxed after a few days in the Paris area, but she knew now she would resume her activities as a "terrorist-at-large". And, more disconcerting, she needed to decide the best way to infiltrate and find her contacts in Algeria and the city of Annaba. Her decision was easy. As soon as she completed her two-plus hour flight from Paris to Annaba, she would make major changes. The change would be much easier, as Alilah Cetin; no more Anglo names such as Darcy Allard in a Muslim country, she concluded. Unless she needed to travel, she would remain Alilah, the credentials given to her two years previously, and by which she was known to Kurt (now AKA Henrik Josephs in North America).

As Alilah planned her next moves in North Africa, Henrik hoped to meet her in Toronto. As he moved toward the security checkpoint in Newark and placed his carry-on bag and briefcase on the conveyer to be scanned, a TSA officer pulled him aside.

"Sir, would you consent to a hand search of your person," said the officer, "We do these checks on a random basis."

"Not a problem," Henrik responded.

"Thank you. Where are you headed today?" asked the officer, "Please step over this way."

"Toronto," said Henrik as he handed his ticket to the agent.

"Thank you. Now, I plan to pat you down lightly. Please raise your arms up to the side. Good," said the officer. The agent patted Henrik down his shoulders, arms, back and legs and then his midsection, thoroughly touching all of his pockets during the procedure. He then used a wand detector to check for metal objects over his entire body.

"Okay, sir, everything seems to be in order. Thank you, and have a nice flight. Sorry for any inconvenience," said the agent.

"No problem," said Henrik

A second agent walked over to the first after Henrik had left the area to go to his departure gate.

"I reviewed his paperwork," said the second agent, "There is no reason to hold this passenger. He has no history anywhere in our records or with Interpol. As you can see, he is not carrying any weapons and has not checked any baggage or brought anything suspicious across the secure area. He is cleared, and I will send that message to the airline."

As Henrik walked briskly to his gate, he thought about purchasing a burner phone and calling Alilah one more time before boarding the flight to Toronto. But he wondered again who might have her phone and what might happen if it rang. He decided to just continue on and try to find her in Canada. He located the gate easily, and within fifteen minutes, the inbound flight arrived on time. Within another thirty minutes Henrik had boarded his plane and settled in for his quick one-hour flight to Toronto. He had not yet planned in detail his next steps.

He knew that Alilah was supposed to fly an Air France jet non-stop to Toronto and arrive about an hour before he had landed in Newark. If she had gone to a hotel, it would be difficult to locate her. On the other hand, if Alilah were in some kind of trouble she may still be at the airport. Their planning had not been precise in large part in their exuberance to leave for North America quickly, but this was really unlike them. Of course, they did not expect to have any issues and they anticipated all along to set up a meeting somewhere in the States.

Upon landing in Toronto, he would first check with the Air France arrivals; if her flight did arrive, he would ask the customer service department if, in fact, Alilah had come to Toronto on that flight. He had no idea if they would comply and provide that information to him. He did not want to raise any suspicions about himself, especially since he had just been questioned and searched before leaving on his own flight.

However, upon landing at the Air Canada terminal, Henrik encountered an immediate problem at the immigration line, and plans changed immediately and unexpectedly. Nothing like this happened when entering the United States.

"What is the problem," Henrik demanded, "I just came from the United States, and had no such problem getting through immigration in Newark."

"Obviously, immigration in the United States did not check you out thoroughly, Mr. Henrik Josephs," the immigration officer responded, "Please follow me over here."

The officer turned the sign in his lane to 'off', and he led Henrik to an office with a door where he would be further interrogated.

"Good afternoon, Mr. Josephs. My name is Donald Moore, I am a senior immigration agent and I have several questions for you. You must answer our inquiries before you may be admitted to Canada, do you understand?" asked Agent Moore.

"Yes, I do. But I do not understand why a delay. Do I represent a threat to your country?" asked Henrik.

"Mr. Josephs, we understand you might have another name, and Josephs is an alias," said Moore.

"I do not know about what you are speaking. My name is Henrik Josephs, just as listed on my papers," said Henrik.

"We have reason to believe that you also have used a different name in several Asian countries. That name is Kurt Huette; does that sound familiar?" asked Agent Moore.

"No, not at all. Where have you obtained this information?" asked Henrik.

"We have this on excellent intelligence from the United States and other international sources, and if you don't admit to this, we have two choices for you. First, we can send you back to the States, where you will be asked the same questions, and I am certain you will be held until their government finds someone who will corroborate this information," said Agent Moore, "or the second choice is the same, there is no second choice you will be going back to the United States, period."

"I can take a polygraph test; I am not this 'Kurt Huette' or whoever you think I am," Henrik demanded.

"That is not an option. Are you Kurt Huette? I have a picture of a man in a seaport that looks like Kurt Huette, and it is your face," said Moore, who was bluffing.

"Okay, yes, I am Kurt Huette; yes, so now what?" said Henrik/Kurt.

"Well Mr. Kurt Huette, that information will get you free transport to One FBI Plaza in Buffalo, NY. They can handle you from there," said agent Moore.

"One more thing Mr. Huette, please tell us the nature of your visit to Toronto."

"I planned on meeting a friend arriving from Paris today," said Kurt, "And, then maybe go to a Maple Leafs game. Do you know where I can get any tickets?"

"Let's get serious sir. Could you please tell us the name of that friend and the airline," said agent Moore.

"Yes, I will cooperate. I have done nothing wrong, and I do not understand the problem. Her name is Alilah Cetin, coming in on an Air Canada flight from Paris," Kurt said.

"I suppose that is a real name?"

"Yes," said Kurt.

"And just to remind you, the reason you are being sent back to the States relates to your travelling under false identity. The FBI and CIA want to question you regarding illegal activities taking place in the United States and overseas; they have an investigative team working on your activities," said Moore, "So you are on your way, and by the way, my assistant just checked; no one by the name of 'Alilah Cetin' entered Canada at any port in the last twenty-four hours. So, I will add that to your list of lies, Mr. Josephs or Huette or whoever you might be. The United States will be aware of this information. Goodbye."

Moore directed his staff to take him immediately on his two-hour drive to the FBI.

"And Mr. Huette, I am so sorry on your first trip to Canada, you will not have an opportunity to see Niagara Falls. You will be passing just a few miles from them. Such beautiful views can be seen from both our side and the American side of this wonder of the world," said Moore as he was led out the door and into a transport vehicle.

After a short, comfortable flight from Paris to Algeria, Alilah deplaned in Annaba. She had absolutely no problem entering the country. The one thing Alilah had thought about during her flight was how to best fit into the Algerian Muslim culture. Having abandoned Muslim clothing, for the most part, the last two years and conservative clothing for many years as an adult, Alilah needed to understand the current garb as well as consider her short-term future and role in the country.

As a woman, she needed to continue to play a leading role in pulling together the global Intifada. Yet, from Alilah's knowledge of Muslim nations, she knew what a difficult task in a male-dominated community this could be for her. It might be a little easier in Algeria. Algerian women did have a greater participation in education than in many other Muslim countries, and with that came a slight uptick in women in the workplace. Alilah hoped moving forward these factors would make it easier for her to work with the men involved in organizing terrorist activities. She thought that it might not yet be the case and could take some time to be on equal footing.

Alilah would need to get by a centuries-old roadblock to make an impact, influence her new male contacts and be able to take on a major role. Women, despite their gains, mostly in the cities, were homebound and continued to play a subservient role to the men in the society and family, especially in North Africa and the Middle East.

When Alilah left the airport, she headed by taxi to the old shopping district, Souk El-Jamaa, in downtown Annaba. From what she saw on the plane and around town, women dressed in a variety of clothing, from full-on burqas and body covering to hijabs and flowing dresses. When walking around the marketplace, she asked a few merchants about the variety of styles women wore. Alilah learned quickly that most city women tended to be more liberal and wore headscarves or hijabs and long skirts, whereas those in the country or in more rural areas often wore burqas and full-body garments.

City women wore a traditional body covering, usually a long, flowing dress called a kaftan, typically made from silk or cotton and decorated ornately. Alilah needed to be confident anywhere and purchased clothing she could wear in any situation.

She took herself and her new purchases by taxi to a downtown hotel. Alilah chose the Sheraton Annaba Hotel since it provided the best security for its mostly American and European clientele. Checking in went smoothly, as several rooms were available in this upscale, expensive location. After resting for just ten minutes or so, Alilah sat back and made her second call on the newly acquired satellite phone. She now knew it was set in the non-

GPS mode, so its location, even though it was not even hers, could never be traced.

Alilah thought about this call before punching in the number. A woman calling a person in Al-Qaeda in the Lands of the Islamic Maghreb, AQIM, would be a rare, if not an unheard-of event. She overcame many obstacles and paid too high a price to get this far to worry about a phone call. She called. A man on the other end answered, and it was exactly the person that the Imam predicted would pick up.

"I expect this is Alilah Cetin, otherwise known as Sabina Mazer," said Abrahim Brahimi, in English quite difficult to understand.

"Yes," said Sabina, "I am Alilah. Thank you for speaking with me. If you prefer to speak in French, we can switch languages. I do not speak Arabic or your native Berber language."

"No, let us continue to speak in English," Abrahim said, "I just wish to tell you I have great respect for your husband, Dr. Mazer, and admiration for you, of course. I am sorry he was captured."

"Thank you for your kind words," she said.

"The Imam told me the work you did to raise money for Dr. Mazer and other activities for the Intifada. You are a shining star among the Muslim women," he said, "But, to lead a war takes strength and courage, and I see this as man's job."

"I think hand-to-hand combat, for the most part, should be a man's job as well. But women have their place in this war. And not just as suicide bombers. I have many strategic ideas; large scale ideas which I think might be useful to discuss with all of our leaders," she said adamantly, "Many of these ideas do not require thousands of men or biological weapons. I know of other mechanisms to bring down strong nations. These are the ideas that need to go before the al-Qaeda and ISIS councils around the world. We cannot act alone as a front here in Africa or the Mideast."

"I am intrigued by your boldness. We are just speaking for the first time, yet you say you have visions of conquering nations without armies. Let us meet soon," Abrahim said, "I will contact you in the next several days and set up arrangements. We can have my men transport you to our location deep in the country near the Atlas Mountain range."

"If you think that is best," she answered, "then let us do it that way. I look forward to hearing back from you." Alilah felt good about the decision and knew that after this brief conversation, an air of mutual respect had developed. Planning for the next phases could begin, and she did not need to worry about Kurt and his plans in the States. She doubted they would come to pass.

32

FBI and CIA Interrogate Huette

2022

Kurt Huette entered the FBI building in Buffalo, escorted by two Canadian immigration officers and was seated on a bench in the entryway. Huette was uncuffed and handed off to an FBI agent, after which the Canadian officers exited the building for their hour-two ride back home.

"Thank you," Kurt shouted back to them as they left, "there was really no need for the handcuffs."

Huette started to complain to the FBI agent that he did not understand why he had been handcuffed. With that, a new set of cuffs was slapped on his wrists. The agent stood him up, led him to an elevator and took him to an interrogation area on another level of the building.

"Mr. Huette, please be seated. I am the senior officer at the Buffalo station of the FBI. My name is Charles Binghamton," said the officer, "I plan to question you on several topics..."

"I will answer as best as I can, but I really do not know why I am here," Kurt broke in.

"Good. Just don't interrupt me again," said Binghamton, "As I began to state, I plan to interrogate you for quite some time on many topics. We have information and evidence that links you to several plots against the United States. For the past two years, many of our enforcement agencies around the country have observed a large increase in bias crimes against Jews, Blacks, Asians, LGBTQ[+] and other groups. In addition, many right-wing activist groups have begun violent activities against these same groups. Let's start with this. Trust me, I have lots more to discuss with you, Mr. Huette," said Binghamton.

"As I told the Canadian authorities, and I will tell you, I have no idea what these allegations have to do with my travels to the United States or Canada," said Huette, "I only came here to meet a friend and see some sights."

"We have received correspondence from Interpol, directly from British Intelligence and the CIA, so we are in a good position to question you on many topics. We shall see if you planned to just do some sightseeing," Binghamton responded, "So first, I want to ask you, would you like some coffee."

"Yes, thank you. It has been a very long day," said Kurt.

"Okay, we will get that for you. Now, tell me what you know about a man named Reverend Jensen," Binghamton demanded.

"Never heard the name," snapped Huette.

"Really, well, I have information from a reputable source that you sent this 'gentleman' start-up fees to begin preaching. You gave him outlines of his sermons to include such erroneous information such as 'Jews killed Jesus, so they must be killed, and Blacks do not have the same cognitive abilities as other races," Binghamton said, "And now, his followers have begun committing violent acts against Jewish and Black people."

"This is not true. You have no proof of this," said Kurt.

"Well, I do have a statement dated two years ago from a bank on the island of Nevis, which we obtained legally. At that time, you paid the Reverend Jensen $10,000. To begin his racist and antisemitic campaign," said Binghamton, "We assume after your initial payment that most of his income and expenses came from local donations."

"Wait one minute. Don't you have laws in this country that prohibit questioning someone before reading some kind of rights?" asked Huette.

"For a first-time traveler to our country, you are pretty smart. You are referring to your Miranda rights, when a person is arrested, 'the right to remain silent, anything you say can be used against you, your right to an attorney, etc.' But, in your case, no!! You see, my questions pertain to crimes that affect public safety and imminent threats," Binghamton responded, "In your case, I can question you without reading you your rights. So, please answer my question: Mr. Jensen seems to be stirring up public problems immediately outside his sermon events, and you funded him. Is that not true?"

"I still do not have to say anything," said Huette.

"Yes. But, we will keep on questioning you without an attorney," said Binghamton, "You and your gang are a threat to the public."

"Okay, I guess you got me there," said Huette.

"Yes, and I believe there might be many more issues that we 'got you' on as well," said Binghamton, "and, oh, here's your coffee, and things may go easier if you begin to cooperate with us."

"Thank you, I really need this now," Huette said.

"As I was saying, before we get into those other areas, right now, as far as I know, you have not yet directly committed any heinous crimes, and you have not been charged with any crimes yet. Yes, we all know you plan to do so and don't get me wrong; we believe many people have already been hurt indirectly by your actions and the actions of your subordinates, especially those working in electronic gaming and pharmaceutical manufacturing facilities overseas. And we will get to that shortly," said Binghamton, "Mr. Huette, we can deal you a fair chance to avoid spending the rest of our life in prison or worse."

"Do I get a lawyer in this country?" asked Huette.

"Well, you certainly can, I just would like to ask you a few more questions," said Binghamton.

"Ask all you wish, but I think I have said enough," said Huette.

"Have it our way. I will ask anyway. First, have you directed any companies and/or employees and/or consultants to those companies to alter the pharmaceutical or biological products imported to the United States?"

"I have no knowledge of that," said Huette.

"Okay, as you wish. Next, have you or anyone associated with you worked with and/or paid the company Gammozunk in Saudi Arabia to develop an online game that pays people to perform real hate crimes?" asked Binghamton.

"I have no knowledge of that," said Huette, "And at this time, I need a lawyer."

"You are correct," said Binghamton, "You do need counsel; your next stop will be in Washington, DC. Tomorrow, you will be flying to our country's CIA headquarters in Langley, Virginia, where I am certain many persons will have questions for you. I have the highest confidence in our Washington agents. They can find you any number of criminal defense attorneys for you to discuss your case and who may wish to represent you. I hope you enjoy your last evening in Buffalo. Good night. My assistant here will find you a comfortable cell for you tonight," with that, Binghamton left the conference room immediately and headed home after a very long day.

Early the next day, Huette boarded a private jet to Washington. It was not his first private jet, but it would turn out to be his last. Upon arrival at CIA headquarters, he had plenty of people to greet him. They all were prepped with questions on multiple topics. First, however, as he had requested, a defense attorney was available to take his case. They met in a private room.

"Mr. Huette, I am aware of some charges that might be made against you today, and others that will be forthcoming," said Conrad Jones, a Federal Defender, "Are you familiar with criminal laws in the United States. I see your original passport is from Senegal as Mr. Josephs, yet I do not have any information about the name 'Kurt Huette'."

"Let me explain, and I am grateful you can represent me. I, Kurt Huette, am a citizen of Iran but am an exile. I have escaped to find freedom," he lied, "many of the activities of which I am accused are solely just related to my attempting to leave Asia and get to the States."

"I see," said Jones, "And these activities include hiring a Revered Jensen to spark racial and antisemitic violence in your escape? I cannot represent a client who will not be truthful with me. I will ask you two other questions. Have you been involved with any persons or companies that might have made alterations to pharmaceuticals or biologic agents imported into the United States?"

"No," Huette said.

"One last question," said the attorney," Have you or anyone you have worked with developed electronic games which convinced individuals to commit real-world bias or hate crimes?"

"No, again, and the FBI asked me these same questions in Buffalo last night," said Huette.

"Mr. Huette, on the contrary, I know of evidence to these allegations. Evidence that came to the United States from an overseas network was presented to me. If you admit to this knowledge or any other such crimes, then I can work with the government to help you," said the attorney, "But, if you continue to stonewall me and others, there is little I can do. We might be able to stop any plots you might have initiated or others that you have not yet revealed."

"I do not know what that means," said Huette, "but I have told you I am from Iran, and I am trying to escape."

"One minute," Jones said, and he left the private interrogation room.

Conrad Jones moved to the Director Erlich's office.

"Director, sir, I think we have a problem. I cannot represent this man," said Jones.

"And why is that," said Erlich.

"I do not believe anything Huette says. He has lied through his teeth," said Jones, "He claims he is seeking asylum from Iran. I have given him the opportunity to come clean, so to speak, and to make a deal with you. I cannot represent him if he lies to me before we start this process."

"So, what is the next step?" said Erlich and Nari said almost simultaneously.

"I have not told him anything about deals that might be made that are not in my hands, and as far as I know, you have not charged him yet," said Jones, the defense attorney, "But right now, public welfare is at risk."

"We need the Attorney General's Office to charge him, and if you refuse to represent him, where do we go to get him his attorney," said Erlich.

Jones said, "Under our Constitution, he has the right to representation; it just will not be me. Get him a lawyer appointed under the Criminal Justice Act. I also suggest making sure he is charged in the next day or two. He cannot be held much longer. Just get him charged and get the prosecutorial process moving forward."

"From what I know from our sources, and since you are not involved as his defense attorney now, Huette has a massive ring of rebel fighters in our nation and around the globe. We need to stop him from initiating any action. Since we have him under arrest, we should use this as leverage. Now is the time to put a major squeeze on him," said Erlich.

"I agree and wish I could help. You need to bring in another attorney today to work with him and get this process moving. Deal now; get the names of everyone in this army or whatever he has out there," said Jones, "If you can do that now, it will be a huge win."

Erlich got right on it. Fortunately, Congress had just passed a law allowing the government to prosecute international war criminal suspects who were in the U.S. irrespective of their nationality. They could then be tried in federal court. Since Huette just happened to be in Virgina, Erlich's office contacted the Justice Department and found an attorney to represent Kurt Huette. Huette was charged with multiple crimes.

Huette was charged with conspiracy to overthrow the government of the United States. He had established a coordinated effort with his generals in several States ready to take action at his command. He used several tactics to gain followers and soldiers, including Reverend Kent Jensen's misguided preachings and the Mean Man Hunt Game, all of which Huette had denied involvement with at first.

Other techniques developed by his generals and lieutenants in the field, including harassment and brutality on citizens, were added to the charges against Huette. The United States Attorney General's office planned to prosecute its case on the protective principle, whereby the United States felt that Huette planned a conspiracy to overthrow the government.

Huette, now faced with unknown consequences of his actions, had choices to make. His newly appointed federal attorney laid it out for him after consulting with the Government.

"Your former attorney, Mr. Jones, did not get very far with you," said his new counsel, "I have some news for you. We have a long way to go here, but start thinking about what you can do to help yourself, avoid a trial and reduce your time in prison in the United States."

"What can I do now?" asked Huette.

"Start pulling together the names of all your leaders in the States and elsewhere; turn off the 'good' Reverend Jensen. You have connections to him and his followers. Who runs the group Liberty Patriots, and who recruits people to their right-wing militia group? The government wants those names. Give up the name of the woman you planned to meet in Toronto. And, in addition, get that game Mean Man Hunt off the internet. Those are the starters," said his attorney.

"If I do those things, can I be set free?" asked Huette.

"Are you joking? No. These are bargaining chips to keep you from remaining in prison here in the United States probably for the rest of your life or the option of being sent back to Iran where your fate may be certain," he said, "Here's a pad of paper. Start writing all that information out. I'll be back."

Erlich, Michael Hardy, and Nari, the CIA team, met briefly with Huette's new attorney. They felt strongly that Huette had no option. Given the prospect of returning to Iran he would have to give up the intelligence. After giving Huette a break of thirty minutes or so, the four of them reconvened with him to see if he had decided to lay down his 'weapons', so to speak. As they entered the conference room, they saw Huette had begun to write but then stopped halfway down the page.

"Mr. Huette, do you have any information for us; your attorney suggested you are willing to bargain with us," said Erlich, the CIA director, "And before we go any further, I am informing you now that these proceedings will be recorded."

"Understood. I began to list some key people in my organization, but then I thought I do not have any assurances…"

"Mr. Huette," Nari Lee broke in, "You will leave for a one-way trip back to Iran if you do not give us a comprehensive list of enemies here in the United States. We suggest, and I am certain your attorney will as well, that you begin talking right now."

"She is correct," interjected Hardy, "so I urge you to give us all your information now; your attorney is here to protect you."

"Yes, Kurt, you do not want to return to face the Government of the Islamic Republic of Iran," said his attorney.

"Alright, I will begin with my generals in the field," and Huette began to rattle off the names of at least 30 men and women. Huette said that each had command of several thousand troops in geographic areas in the States and only acted upon his command. Both Erlich and Hardy recognized a few of the names as ex-high-ranking U.S. military commanders and struggled with this information.

"Tell us about the control these generals have over the "troops" and the arms available for what appears to be an insurrection," said Nari.

"I expect my command has complete control, and over the past twenty years, we have accumulated sufficient weapons to accomplish our goals," said Huette.

"Who is your second in command?" asked Erlich.

"That individual is not in the United States," answered Huette.

"My question was who, not where," repeated Erlich.

"I apologize, but I cannot and will not divulge that information," Huette said.

"Is your second in command a female," asked Nari.

"What's the difference? That only eliminates half the population," Huette joked.

"Well, since you do not feel like providing us answers to all our questions, we feel obligated to send you back where you belong. Justice will be served. But first a few more questions," said Erlich, "Maybe you will answer these. First, do you have anyone who can turn off the Mean Man Hunt game?"

"Yes, I have access to the manufacturer in Saudi Arabia," he said, "I can convince them to shut it down."

"Good, now two right-wing propaganda groups growing at exponential rates are linked to you. One, Reverend Kent Jensen and his followers have begun to shake up small towns and commit acts of violence. You need to turn him off," said Michael Hardy.

"And a second group," added Nari, "Liberty Patriots, a seemingly normal group, actually recruits people to its right-wing group but is a very organized militia operation."

"Yes, I can get to both of these groups, but what's been started cannot be stopped," said Huette.

"That's a damn shame," said Erlich, "Maybe we can make Mr. Huette an example of what might happen if actions are taken against our nation…."

"I think you need to tread lightly here, Mr. Erlich," said Huette's attorney, "Up until now, you have been just asking for information as part of a deal; now you are making a threat. That is enough."

"Fine, no more threats. I apologize," said Erlich, "I believe the CIA has obtained sufficient information to act upon. However, we have one final question for Mr. Huette."

"Yes, I will follow up," said Nari, "You entered Canada as a 'Henrik Josephs', correct?"

"Correct."

"Why did you falsify your identity?" asked Nari.

"Simply this, as you can understand from what we discussed, my operation to engage in a battle with the United States requires cover," said Huette, "That is all."

"The woman you claimed to be meeting, according to notes from Canadian Immigration, was someone named 'Alilah Cetin'. Was that also a cover?" asked Nari.

"No, she was a friend I planned to meet, but I guess she never got to Canada," Huette said.

"Alright, thank you for your forthright answers," Nari said with a sardonic smile.

"I think that just about concludes our questioning for now. Thank you, Mr. Huette," said Erlich, "We will speak with your attorney and the Attorney General's Office before communicating the next steps in your legal proceedings."

With that, Huette was returned to a holding cell in CIA headquarters. His future was indeterminate. Would he stay in the United States and never see freedom again, or be shipped back to Iran and face worse consequences? At least for now, the Government had made major inroads into stopping a major rebellion and slowing the surging hate and hate mongers rising in the country and possibly elsewhere.

33

End of the Beginning

Autumn 2022

Nari continued to follow closely the research on the expression of the Bornavirus p24 protein. When the central nervous system tissue from individuals who died after receiving the aberrant measles vaccine was analyzed by Dr. Allison Bailey at USAMIIRD in Frederick, MD, Nari's hypothesis proved correct. Pieces of the p24 protein were found in the brains of these children and teens who had developed aberrant behavior. The suicides, the anorexia, and the aberrant behaviors all showed up in one or two groups of young persons. The FDA's original finding of RNA for the Bornavirus protein in the MVoneshot vaccine clearly demonstrated intent to harm the population.

These two pieces of information, which Nari Lee put together, led to two major areas of follow-up investigation. First, an attempt to locate all those vaccinated children started and second, development of a treatment to either prevent the expression of the Bornavirus p24 protein in the body or neutralize its effect.

She sensed that finding the recipients of the vaccine would be an easy task. Most states, at least in the U.S., maintained centralized vaccination records. However, having worked in the biotech industry, Nari also knew that pharmacies and wholesalers also had records of injections and shipments. From there, individual patient tracking could be accomplished in an emergency. In the end, all vaccine recipients in the U.S. could be found. The European agents could do the same.

The second goal, finding a treatment, which started a year before, took on a "Manhattan Project" like approach. The NIH and several biotechnology companies engaged in pursuit of a cure. Scientists knew at the outset that the target for treatment, the brain, would be difficult. Further, most thought that the cure would require getting a large biological agent into the brain to neutralize this p24 protein or RNA.

The blood-brain barrier, or BBB, became the issue. The BBB protects the relatively normal brain from unwanted substances getting into the brain from the outside. Normally, this is a good thing. But the BBB needs to be tricked to get a large foreign molecule into the brain to treat a disease.

As months passed, more and more teens were placed in therapy for psychiatric disorders or early signs of problems in order to prevent self-harm or harm to others. Time started to run out. Biotechnology companies poured more of their own resources and government money into developing a treatment for children who had the Bornavirus RNA activated in their brains. The BBB problem still had not been overcome, but two promising candidate treatments made their way to the FDA to obtain approval for testing in humans. It had been almost a year, and in most categories of developments, this was 'light speed'.

The most sophisticated, RNAi, was a "killer RNA". RNA in the cell normally helps to make the body's proteins. In this case, the RNAi (inhibitory RNA) would turn off the bad Bornavirus RNA that sat in the brain and was needed to make the p24 protein, which caused the brain problems.

The RNAi therapy, in theory, would bind to the Bornavirus RNA as the cell makes it and block it. Then there would be no production of the p24 protein, and the problem would be solved. But no company could figure out a way to get past the BBB. It needed some kind of stabilizing carrier because once it got into the blood, it would be torn apart by enzymes and useless.

An Indian company developed a liposome technology, basically a "bag of fat", so that the RNAi could slip into the fatty brain tissue and do its thing. The company then tested its product on chimpanzees, and it reversed the behavior issues in the infected animals. Although chimp studies were not performed to check to see if the drug material could cross a "normal" brain, the FDA decided a small test study in older teens who already had symptoms would be acceptable in order to determine if the drug had some activity.

Once the FDA approved the pilot or small study in the older teens who already had symptoms to evaluate, parents clamored to have their children enrolled. Only thirty patients, including five from India, were allowed to be entered, and it took less than one week to fully enroll the study.

The observation period of the study, eight weeks, did not give the product enough time to fairly evaluate long-term adverse effects. However, within three months from start to finish, all the data had been collected, and no significant problems or adverse events were observed.

Based upon the results of this small study, a larger, 500-patient, 16 weeks, multinational study designed. It would determine if the RNAi would be safe and effective in preventing or treating neurologic damage in those who received the MVoneshot vaccine.

In the meantime, two manufacturing facilities, one in India and a second larger facility in Virginia, risk manufactured supplies on a large scale for the market. In the hope that the trials proved successful, the treatment would be ready to go as soon as the FDA and other agencies approved the product for the market. Both facilities began to manufacture sufficient supplies for the market.

Enrollment, usually the most difficult part of the clinical trial process, proceeded without a glitch. After all the clinical investigative sites met by video conference to review the study, and it was approved by committees at the sites, all 500 patients were enrolled in two months. The wheels of research could not have moved any faster, and within 6 months, the study was completed.

One month later, the analyses and preliminary report were complete and sent to the FDA and other worldwide agencies. The treatment not only slowed, it stopped the progression of any neurologic disease. No significant safety issues could be detected within the study period; however, the FDA insisted that subjects be followed long-term to monitor adverse events.

After a quick and thorough review, the FDA gave the product an Emergency Use Approval for anyone who had received the modified MVoneshot vaccine, whether or not they displayed symptoms. The European equivalent of the FDA, the EMA, and the CDSCO in India similarly provided emergency approvals. Full approval would never be needed since the initial vaccine was withdrawn from the market and would never be administered again. In any case, the FDA asked the NIH to develop a patient registry and follow 20,000 asymptomatic subjects who received the vaccine in order to determine long-term safety and clinical information.

In short, the RNAi product was released in the U.S. by a Cambridge, Massachusetts-based firm, Universe Biotechnology, partnering with the Indian company for the overseas market. The U.S. company had no other products in its pipeline beyond the early development stage. This limited use of the RNAi product for the 575,000 or so patients who received the MVoneshot vaccine provided no real revenue stream for Universe Biotechnology. The U.S. government took on all liability for the product and also granted a no-strings-attached government award of $10,000,000 for the Company to continue their work in this field of research.

Such a windfall not only helped stretch out the Company's ability to survive as an entity but also raised its visibility with investors. Since there had been problems with drug alteration around the world and in the U.S., the NIH, FBI and CIA handled the oversight of manufacturing and worldwide distribution of the product. In the meantime, Immunoviratherapeutics, once a high flyer on the NASDAQ with its two vaccines, had been delisted from the stock exchange and worth pennies.

The former CEO, officers and board of directors were inundated with both class action and individual liability lawsuits for the distribution of its harmful MVoneshot vaccine. Dr. Alan Mazer, fighting his own civil lawsuits, sat in prison and was glad not to be associated directly with the Company.

In any case, he knew his life would remain the same, whatever the result of these lawsuits. This god-forsaken prison in the woods of Virginia was his home for the rest of his life, and he knew he deserved it. He only hoped that his children would not suffer financial liability for his crimes.

"You have pulled together some excellent information on this case," said Erlich, "nice job for a newbie."

"Well, I guess that proves I belong behind a desk at Langley," Nari surmised, "I luckily came upon enough clues to at least determine the root cause of one source of the huge uptick in violence we had seen," Nari said.

Martin Erlich remarked, "We've just begun. The Agency now has a worldwide net and significant intelligence out there to find and capture Sabina Mazer/Alilah Cetin and her collaborators. Nari, you suspected she worked with Kurt Huette. You brought so much to this investigation. I know this will be up to Michael, but your sitting behind a desk won't help us find these terrorists. We have people that can track the basic movements of whomever we discover," Erlich continued, "If we need your expertise, I will recall you to a station or to Langley. For now, it is my hope that you will be back in the field."

"You are the Director, sir," said Nari, "if you think I will better serve the Agency and country chasing shadows, then I will be on my way. Just please make sure I have satellite access to the fastest internet service available as I wind around mountain roads looking for Sabina and her insurgents."

Nari rose from her chair, gave the Director Erlich a smile, and left his office. Erlich knew that in her heart Nari yearned for another field experience despite her prior close encounter with death. He thought maybe there would be hope for a world to carry on in peace.

Author's Note

We Are All The Same, Really

What began several years ago in my novel <u>Invisible Threat</u> as one way to confront anti-vaxxers has now evolved. In that book, the case was made for proper and timely vaccination when thousands of children died at the hands of a terrorist who purposely developed a harmful vaccine. The theme shifts in <u>We Can't Go Back</u> to war against hatred. This novel picks up on characters from my first novel and adds to them a mix of new bigoted and eccentric personalities. These individuals demonstrated a hatred of Jews, Blacks, Asians, LBGTQ$^+$ and others. They develop sickening means of threatening and damaging these people in order to gain plans for world domination.

Just like viruses, I believe that hate also requires a vaccine. Hate and prejudice are similar to virus infections. Virus infections start with one or a few persons and then spread to their closest contacts. From there, it spreads and spreads, and finally, over time, it's out of control. Now, the same can be said of the concept of hate for an individual or group. It does not take much for a few individuals to spread rhetoric, contempt and lies about a group of people.

Once this happens, and negative events become associated with this group, then more and more people begin to question the good of this group and start to disassociate from them. With motivation by a leader or government, soon most will start to distrust these people, and before long a hatred will develop. These types of events can and do happen. The Jewish people were close to eliminated in the most recent and extreme case in Nazi Germany. In recorded history, as many as 34,000,000 people have been killed by genocide.

Antisemitism did not begin in World War 2. The Jewish people have been targeted by hate since before the common era. After being slaves in Egypt and led from captivity by Moses, hardship continued. Their population grew in great numbers only to be slaughtered again by Romans in two wars. In the Middle Ages, again, Jews were persecuted, blamed for plagues, expelled, and killed throughout Europe. The Inquisition continued for almost 500 years in Central and South America.

Experiments have shown that hate can be prevented with education. On the other hand, children pick up on clues from the environment at the youngest of ages. If parents and family show prejudice, it will be learned. It all starts early. Education begins in the first years of childhood, and behavior and attitude can only change with a concerted effort.

The analogy of the spread of infection and hate can be taken a step further and is terrifying. Throughout history, almost a billion people have been killed at the hands of monstrous dictators, by genocide and war, and close to the same number have died by pandemics and epidemics. We have now developed vaccines or treatments against many of the deadly infectious diseases. The best vaccine to protect us against hate and subsequent war is education and tolerance of others. Graham Nash, of Crosby, Stills, Nash and Young, in his 2013 autobiography, stated that the lyrics to "Teach Your Children Well" refer to the fact that if we don't teach our kids ways to deal with each other, humanity won't survive.

Finally, we have all heard that we are all the same when cut away under the skin. We are also all related. [1] If one goes back as recently as 55 AD, all of us are descended from someone who was alive at that time.[1] Go back a little further, somewhere around 2,500 to 5000 BCE and you get to what the author of the article refers to as the 'genetic isopoint'. This is where the family trees of any two people on earth trace back to the same set of individuals, no matter how distantly related. So, as much intolerance and hatred as there might exist, we are all one. The key to stopping bigotry begins in the mind and heart. You have your own vaccine, use it, "teach your children well".

This novel, my second, was written largely before the increase in antisemitic hate crimes in 2023 and 2024 and well before the October 7 Hamas attack on The State of Israel. Jews are the most targeted religious group, comprising only 2% of the U.S. population, yet targets of 60% of religiously motivated hate crimes, according to FBI data. (Security Community Network, 12-Oct-2023). Since October 7, 2023 there have been 10,000 antisemitic incidents in the U.S. (6-Oct- 2024 Antidefamation League Press Release).

1. Hershberger, S. (2020, October 5). Humans are all more closely related than we commonly think. *Scientific American.*

If you have enjoyed this book, please leave a review on Amazon or Goodreads and recommend it to a friend.